Maria Beale

Jack O'Doon

A Novel

Maria Beale

Jack O'Doon
A Novel

ISBN/EAN: 9783337032098

Printed in Europe, USA, Canada, Australia, Japan

Cover: Foto ©Andreas Hilbeck / pixelio.de

More available books at **www.hansebooks.com**

JACK O'DOON

A Novel

BY

MARIA BEALE

NEW YORK
HENRY HOLT AND COMPANY
1894

JACK O'DOON.

CHAPTER I.

A N old man stood on a pier head, scanning the sullen water and lowering sky. He was dressed in the rough garb of a fisherman, and his clothes hung loose upon his bent figure. A boatswain's silver chain was about his neck and the whistle was in his hand ; silent now, but he held to the habits of his youth in the infirmity of his age.

He knew the portent of the leaden clouds whose shaggy edges dragged upon the black waters ; of the curling foam, which the incoming tide, with each repeated breaker, lifted higher upon the sand ; and he groaned as he turned at last dejectedly away and followed the shore to a hut, where the pale blue smoke, as it fell to the earth, told of a fireside within which was warmed against the cold and damp without.

Having reached the door, he looked again across the bay, and, by the light of the yellow line around the sky, saw the far-off "surf-horses" tossing on the harbor bar. The channel was so narrow, the shoals so many, it would be grounding and death to ride that foaming line to-night; and, shuddering because of his aching heart, he entered the low door and closed it behind him.

"Could you see nothing, father?" asked a woman anxiously, for one of their sons, the latest born, was mate of a ship which had not come in; and the father was picturing it as beaten about with rudderless hull and riving masts; with ragged sails and snapping shrouds; without stay or brail on a sky-bound sea.

"The Lord ha' mercy!" cried he, flinging out his arms in misery. A moment later he loosened the knot of his yarn comforter as if it choked him. He was so old that the energy of hope was dead, and there was no strength in him save that of terror. Terror of inky waves torn for ragged shrouds! Terror for battered hulks scuttling down! "O Lord, Lord, ha' mercy, an' pity my boy!" he cried with such appeal it sounded like authority. The woman was silent, though she heard distinctly enough the surging of the waves. She knew the breakers were rising high and hollow when they fell with such lumbering crashes upon the beach. The old planks in the door rattled as if a hand had shaken them, and the wind rose higher, and shrieked dismally in the chimney, as if ghosts of

drowned sailors from all the seas of the world
had come, like an innumerable army of martyrs,
to warn these poor and very old people of the
bad news some one was bringing.

So it sounded to the woman who stood
pressing her hands upon her temples in
dread. Then she rallied her courage and
listened. The fire was sputtering. She put
together the charred logs, and the salt rime
scintillated. She had more hope than the
man ; it was natural she should have, since
the history of those things we hear does not
remain with us like the vision of those which
we see ; and there was a wonderful tenderness in her manner of wiping a tear from her
husband's cheek, and a vast resource of fortitude behind the calmness with which, out of
her own self-control, she strove to inspire confidence in the man, who was older and feebler
than herself. But no cheer was in him. As
they sat silent in the gloom of the smoulder-
ing fire, the wrinkles and furrows, sunken
deep in their faces, told the story of their hard-
working and weather-beaten lives ; and suggested in the career of the man bleak nights
at sea on a pilot station, cold late springs on
the foggy banks of the mackerel fisheries,
and numb and almost devitalized watches
aloft, when the morning sometimes found one
missing and gone to a gruesome grave. A
sad relief no doubt from the pinch of living.

Harassed by such memories, the old man
envied the pilot, Jack Gavely, in that the

Lord had spared him much by taking him in time ; and in sorrow he sighed and wished to the Lord that he too were dead. The woman understood him, and, conscience-smitten, endeavored to cheer him by making the fire blaze. The kindling flame illuminated the interior of the hut. There was a strange commingling from land and sea on all sides. Around the walls were fragments of canvas, mildewed to a tender gray ; others, red with tannin as Ionian sails. In a corner, like a gilded trophy, or a fetish turned to gold, was the battered, but still gaudy figurehead of a brig which the waves had sent for a votive offering. A cupboard was near it with a white and gilded door ; and a china door-plate, bearing the words, "Gentlemen's Smoking-room."

The joists overhead were made from ships' spars and were black with smoke, which often, as now, blew down the chimney in gusts. Bunches of seaweed, pink and yellow, hung from the beams ; and all the crannies in the walls were filled with small marine monstrosities, such as sea-urchins and starfish ; and little crabs, hung by threads, wriggled in the streams of wind which came puffing through the cracks. It was a living habitation, compiled from fragmentary evidences of death ; made, in all its parts, from the debris of wreckage, which the sea had rejected and the salvage hunters despised. There was a faint delicious smell from the

cupboard, where a piece of Malabar sandal-
wood was used to close a crevice. On one
side of the cabin was the imperfect outline of
a huge number 9, which, though battered and
worn, stood out as unmistakable as when, on
the high seas, it had signaled to the good ship
the pilot, ready to steer her in. There was
a clock, too ; but its wooden wheels, warped
by the fogs, refused to run ; and a peg, by
the shadow that it flung, told the hours when
the sun shone.

In the daytime the outside of the hut
appeared as quaint as the inside. It was
crouched under a dune, and the shifting sand
was slowly encasing it. The low chimney
seemed only a hole in the hill from which a
wreath of smoke issued. The front of the
little shanty was much pluckier, however,
and put a bold face to the sea ; and never a
gale, though it blew hard from the northeast,
had had power to loosen its roof of mixed
wood, tin, and tarpaulin, nor to tear off one of
the many-colored boards, as varied as Joseph's
coat, with which it was sided. There was a
space which had been blue and bright as
the skies in summer, another as green as a
meadow in spring, and a great dash of scarlet ;
and interspliced among these were yellow,
brown, black and white. But all, motley as
was the mixture, were weather-beaten till
they had acquired a film of gray, which made
them tender to the sight.

It was, indeed, a queer little house, yet you

could not fail to see it. So small compared with the white-capped sea, and so small compared with the hillocked sand ; buried in white sheets, it looked like a toy-house, which a child had taken to bed in its arms, and had run away and forgotten in the morning.

But you must have seen it, as you would see an eye in a reposeful face, for it was the eye in the vast speechless face of nature there ; the one spot, of all the sky, water, and land, where life and soul were. That night, however, the darkness was dense.

The old couple within had no heart to eat, although the woman had filled the kettle and spilled her tears into it as she put it on the crane. She had brushed them away as she laid the cloth, and set out the dishes, and busied herself to make the potatoes boil ; but when they were served, she forgot the supper, and the kettle spluttered and steamed in vain, until it nearly put out the fire. Just then there came a hesitating knock, a timid lifting of the latch, followed by the wrenching of the door from the grasp of a small hand which held it, and the inrush of a gust of wind, bringing sand and sea-spray along with it. Both were startled, and arose, confronting the unexpected visitor.

" May the Lord bless us ! " exclaimed the astonished old man. The gale was so fierce that it took the combined strength of all three to close the door against it. Having done so, they barred it from within.

The figure which had entered was that of a woman. She approached the fire, and, kneeling down on the hearth, in the space they made for her, proceeded to put the brands together and kindle a blaze. The hands which she stretched out to the warmth were delicate and well cared for, and sparkled with rings ; and one would have thought the wearer strangely out of place, wandering alone, on such a night, in such a storm, amid darkness and danger.

She had set upon the table a double-glazed hurricane lamp.

"What's fetched you here, Mercy, when the wind's a-tarin' the sand-hills down, en flingin' 'em into the sea like ez no. It mus' be bad news you's bringin' us, sence you got nothin' to say," said the woman, in great anxiety.

At first the girl did not reply, and the silence was ominous. At length, after vainly trying to speak, she burst out sobbing, and buried her face in her foster-mother's lap, for she had come to bring her grief.

The old man clasped his hands under his chin, and swayed his body from side to side, with the necessity of an active nature for mechanical expression ; but the woman was dumb. No tear, nor sigh, nor heaving of the breast, marred the rigidity of her desolation. She looked as if she were dead herself, while the girl, regaining her composure, arose from her knees and sat down with her feet to the fire.

The hood which she pushed back from her face was lined with fur, and her cloak was also of the same rich material ; and, as she sat thus, the eyes of her two companions turned inquiringly upon her, watching her draw from her pocket a newspaper, slowly unfold it, and, with a voice tremulous and interrupted with tears, read as follows :

"Yesterday, at noon, the bark Junaluska of the Currituck Fisheries' service arrived, towed into port by the tug Annie. She was helplessly dismantled, having lost her mast-heads, shrouds and sheets. Her rudder also was missing. Still, we are glad to say that her crew, save one seaman, Jacob Billings by name, is intact ; but she brings sad news of her sister bark, the Marianetta, Captain Freemantle, mate John O'Doon, which, when last sighted, was listed beyond hope of righting, and, without spars or masts, was thought to be sinking when night came on. This was on Thursday last, the thirtieth of March. The next morning there was nothing to be seen of her, although the sun rose clear, and if she were still afloat it is thought she might have been sighted. She was drifting S. S. W. No hopes are entertained for the safety of the crew, as the tempestuousness of the night, the frightful roughness of the sea, and the smallness of the boats make it difficult to conceive how any could have lived through it. The marine insurance companies sent out a tug in search, which, having returned with but one of the missing boats, they are inclined to give the Marianetta up as lost."

The paper sank upon the girl's lap and she clasped her hands over it.

" But surely she might have drifted many miles in a night. Fifty miles with such a wind ! Oh, *he must be alive.* Dear Jack !" cried she, in such sincere and bitter grief, that the old father looked at her in wonder ere he replied with a retrospective frown,—

"Yes, and be a-starvin', and a-freezin' to death, off'n the shoals o'Cape Hatteras to-night. No. Better dead, say I, and over with, than sech a sufferin', livin', an' dyin' all at once ! Oh, I knows ! I've know'd it, and I'd ha' blessed the good Lord to ha' deadened en a-drownded me with a big stunnin' header at once."

But the youth and hope in the girl resisted, and clung to the thought that none had seen him die ; and the mother, stimulated by the example of one hoping beside her, felt her heart warm a little.

" Dear Jack," murmured the girl gently, "I can't remember anything without him. Nobody was ever half as good except you and daddy," and she turned to the old woman with a caress which touched her. Sidewise to the fire, her profile was distinct against the light. The forehead was high and noble, but the apparent height was diminished by the hair which clung to it in wet ringlets. It was not a symmetrical face, but a kindly one ;

and the chin, though rather broad, was rounded
into a throat of great beauty. Her head, a
trifle large, was well set upon her shoulders,
as one discovered when she unhooked the
silver clasps and spread her cloak over the
back of her chair.

"And how was it you got here to-night?"
inquired the man, shifting his anxiety to the
girl; for, now that the worst had come, he
roused himself to meet it.

"I came alone," said she simply. It did
not strike her that there was anything heroic
in crossing the sand-dunes by a familiar path
which she had so often trodden since first
her infant feet had toddled along it, clinging
to her foster-mother's dress. But the old man
shook his head dubiously.

"You might ha' lost the road; en afore now
the sands is drefted over the bushes mor'n'
you can make 'lowance fur. You'll stay here
to-night, 'longside o' the ole ooman. She'll
stow ye to le'ward an' I'll set here afore the
fire tell mornin'."

The girl hesitated a moment and looked
at her watch. "It is eleven o'clock," said
she. "They will not miss me. I said I should
go to bed after father had brought the news,
and I did undress and sit down by the fire in
my room; but at last I could not bear it by
myself any more, and so I dressed again and
came down quietly, and lighted the lantern,
and went out to try the path, and finally I got
here; for after I once started I hated to stop,

and I kept behind the hillocks when I could. But several times the wind blew me down, and I had to carry the lantern under my cloak when I faced it. It seems strange the sand doesn't drift over you altogether, these nights."

" It will," said the old man with conviction, " when me en the ole ooman is dead, en there ain't no person to dig it away ; en now ez Jack is drownded, en he's the last o' our crew, I's been a-tellin' her there ain't nar'a fittener place fur her en me ter bide in. Jes roll us two up in our blankets, en shet to the door, en let her dreft. She's a fair ole craft, she be." He looked round upon the curious walls with satisfaction. " An' arter the door is shet, the sand'll purty soon close her down. I've a mind, as ye won't find nar'a spot es consecrated fur us, Mercy, ez this here. There ain't none o' our childurn now to come back. They was born here, one by one, but they's all foun' another cradle, what'll rock 'em without gittin' tired, and sing 'em ter sleep nights forever ! "

The pathos in the old man's voice smote the mother's heart into a great lamentation. " Rachel weeping for her children, and would not be comforted, because they were not." The girl hung upon her, and entreated her, with the persuasion of innumerable caresses, to cease from her sorrow and crying, but without avail ; and at last she sat down again beside the old man, and they listened to the

mother's heart outpouring. It was awful to
hear, for it seemed as if it were breaking;
and yet they were too wretched to comfort
her; and so they sat listening and gazing
blindly into the fire. Occasionally the man
groaned when the wind rushed down the
chimney, and reminded him of the fierceness
of the storm upon the sea. The canvas
flapped against the wall with a startling noise;
and the sand came rattling down in blasts
and scattered over them. It was indeed drifting over the little house, smothering the chimney more and more.

All was making an indelible impression
upon the girl, despite the fact that her courage was so strong. It is true she had been
brought up to the lullaby of the sea; but
since the time when the sorrows of shipwreck
could be understood, she had been sheltered
behind the massive walls of her father's house,
where even the plate-glass windows were so
strong and tight, that, when doubled in winter,
only the booming of a great storm could be
heard distinctly. But the grandeur of old
Margery O'Doon's fortitude, in her little hut
by the sea, had won from the girl an admiration all the greater because of the contrast
between their lots in life, and altogether apart
from her natural instinct of love for her foster-
mother.

Old Margery's courage had never been
known to falter, though her sons had been
brought in, wrinkled and drowned and dead,

all soaked with sea-water, and laid at her feet.
She had not shrunk from fulfilling for them
the last sad offices, and herself had shrouded
them for the grave.

Knowing them both so well, and having
seen that day that their hearts were dying
of suspense, this girl had crossed the sands
through the darkness to bring them evil tid-
ings, believing that certainty, even of the
worst, were better than the dread which was
maddening them.

Jack O'Doon, the last of seven sons who
had gone down to the sea in ships, was the
pride and glory of his mother's heart. She
had called him her scholar, and now, seeing
his books, with his name upon them, in a bold
and clerkly hand, arose, and, with a desperate
necessity for expression, kissed them with
idolatrous fervor again and again. "My
boy, my boy!" she cried, wringing her hands,
"he won't come back no more." The girl
looked on, but her eyes were dry; she had
not realized it yet. She had not had that
tuition of disappointment which at last teaches
us to shrink from the most casual separation,
as we shrink from death; and so she sat with
a mute and reverent sympathy, following
Mother Margery with her eyes, unconscious
of the strong contrast between herself and
her old nurse.

Even her clothes were so different from
Mother Margery's. Her dress was thick and
warm, and was cut with the precision of

fashion ; her rings were too costly for her years ; and her hair was twisted upon a gold pin. One was a petted child ; the other was a brave old woman whose lot had been severe, and whose burden was very heavy. But, without knowing it, the girl had been nourished with courage, as well as milk, from her foster-mother's breast, and that night she showed it, for it took a wonderful endurance to sit through the dark hours till the fickle April sun shone in the morning.

CHAPTER II.

N the early light the girl returned to her father's house, and, reaching her room, threw herself upon the bed and fell asleep.

She was the darling and only child of a re-tired sea-captain, the offspring of his strangely-assorted marriage with the daughter of an impecunious Episcopal clergyman, accredited with more learning than money. The mother died in giving birth to the child. Usually under such circumstances, when the father re-covers from the shock of his bereavement, he either detests the innocent cause of his mis-fortune, or else overwhelms it with more than the usual quality and quantity of affection. This erstwhile mariner, Solomon Blessington, better known in those parts as "The Captain," having amassed a fortune, had abandoned his life upon the slippery wave at the age of thirty-eight and established himself on shore, full of hope and lavish of expenditure. Not con-tent with giving his refined young wife all that money could buy for her, he had settled an annuity upon each of her sisters, and been altogether so bountiful to the parson, his father-in-law, that many, who could not reconcile themselves to this marriage of " Beauty and the Beast," had declared it looked as if the old monster had bought the girl, out and out.

But when a woman has found life cold and poverty bitter, she is often content to yield herself without reserve to even violent passion, provided it is tender and sheltering; and I am inclined to think that the Captain's wife felt such trust in his goodness as made her ignore—even perhaps fail to see—his coarseness.

Taking the world as it is, poverty, even though ameliorated by scholarly culture, without leisure for enjoyment, finds it hard to withstand the seductions of food and clothes, abundance of resources for the gratification of one's near kin, and general peace of mind ; provided the heart be free to make the sacrifice.

But in this case, if sacrifice there had been, doubtless the mother's secret brooding over it had had much to do with shaping the future inclinations of the then unborn child, and creating those germs of a character so out of keeping with her surroundings ; for, having inherited her father's energy and large-minded generosity, her mother's self-abnegation, and her grandfather's devotion to abstract study, her inherent tendencies continually rebelled against Aunt Polly's severe discipline and narrow ideas.

At the end of the first eight years of her

life, which had been passed under the tender care of Mother Margery and Jack, the parson saw fit to shuffle off this mortal coil, leaving the coil to Aunt Polly in the shape of aggressive fanaticism. The Captain, in view of his sister-in-law's desolation, had thought it best to transplant her to Blessington House, and put her in charge of his child.

Mercy's little hands were henceforth washed of the defilement of frog-houses and sea-fiddlers, and a change came over the spirit of her dreams. She was set down to tasks and lessons day by day. On Sunday she was harnessed without pity to the religious treadmill, and Aunt Polly, a remorseless prig, made a prig of the child as well.

The infant heart had had veins of gold to withstand the unbounded indulgence of her father, and the purse-proud arrogance which had undermined Aunt Polly's common-sense on the sudden accession of fortune.

* * * * *

When the girl awoke and descended to the breakfast-room, her father was off again to town, and Aunt Polly, a grim person with eye-glasses, sat deeply engrossed in religious literature ; marking sentences with a lead pencil as she hurriedly scanned the pages, her thin lips pinched in the eagerness of pursuit.

Mercy abhorred *tracts*.

" I have been looking up a few things for

2

Margery," said Aunt Polly, pointing to a pile
of pamphlets.   .

"I never could see any sense in that sort of
thing," said Mercy, "and I hope you won't
read them to Mother Margery to-day. She
must feel as if she doubted heaven and earth,
and wished she were dead!"

"Why, what possesses you?" cried Aunt
Polly, looking at Mercy.

"I don't know," replied the girl, putting a
lump of sugar into her coffee, "but it seems
to me there can't be much worse hereafter
than tossing about on a pitch-black sea, starving and freezing and dying, and I wish Jack
had never been born!"

"Pray, do not speak in that wild way,
Mercy," said Aunt Polly, putting up her glasses
to scrutinize her niece.

"I am not talking in a wild way! I can't
get along without Jack. He's mine, and I
want him," Mercy retorted, abandoning her
breakfast and coming round to face her aunt,
who, with a faint color in her cheeks, was still
perusing the tracts.

"It is a wild way," she replied, without
looking up, "because, in the first place, you
are not treating me with proper respect, and
in the second, it does not become you to be
rhapsodizing over a person no better than a
servant."

The girl's face, already vivid with emotion,
turned scarlet with anger. She stood for a
moment silent, and then, leaning forward, said

with a low emphasis which surprised her aunt,
"Yes, he was my father's servant. He gave
his courage, and endurance, and youth, and
strength, and perhaps his life, for the wretched
pay of thirty dollars a month and found. And
he was my slave too. A dumb slave, always,
since we played in the old boat on the beach
together! But he was my benefactor as well;
and I loved him for both, and I'll miss him for
both!" The anger had suddenly died out of
her voice, and it had sunk to so low a key
that the fervor of its tenderness alone made it
audible.

Aunt Polly had lived through too much
poverty, and had struggled too long and too
indomitably to keep up a vestige of family
dignity, not to feel grave annoyance at Mercy's
staunch loyalty to the O'Doons. She glanced
at the girl, and, knowing how incorruptible
was her devotion, deemed it best to let the
subject drop, and said, as if to close the interview, "Such things are better forgotten than
talked about; but I shall certainly go to the
O'Doons."

"Have a little pity, and do not torment
them with those things!" cried the girl,
throwing herself in her aunt's way, in an
attitude of entreaty. "Is there nothing in
your heart you can give them?—*nothing?*"

It was an unusual scene. Mercy appeared
in a new character before her aunt, who could
but look at her in wonder, and in sheer surprise let the tracts flutter to the ground; for

there was such determination to defend Mother Margery at any cost, that Mercy showed the spirit of a young tigress over its wounded dam.

Aunt Polly gazed at the bits of paper on the floor as if she expected a lambent glimmer to play round them and proclaim their inspiration ; Mercy looked at them as though she longed to put them through a crucial test and throw them into the fire.

At length, with a fainting feeling, the girl sank into a chair, and, covering her face with her handkerchief, wept as if she had lost the dearest friend she possessed in the world, and had neither hope nor expectation beyond what had passed away.

Aunt Polly, with a resolute intention of having her own way, stooped down, gathered up the tracts, and, looking at Mercy with a slight commiserating smile, left her. She, poor child, was glad to be alone. The hope which had resisted the depression of the night now failed her ; and the memory of the reluctance which the old sailors always evinced at seeing their young ones go out on the smacks during the gusty March weather came grim and hard upon her, and she made no allowance for the cowardice of age so sickened by bitter experience as to forget the endurance of youth.

She fell into one of the "brown studies" for which Aunt Polly was forever chiding her. Her mind was tenacious and analytical, and

having nothing to interest it socially, philoso-
phized upon all she observed and hoarded
until she could sit by the sea in summer and
the fireside in winter, to think out causes and
relations.   It was this habit of casuistry which
gave her so full an insight into the character
of the O'Doons, mother and son.   She was a
problem to her father and Aunt Polly, who
could not certainly decide if she were a genius
or a fool ; since somebody claims that absent-
minded persons must be one or the other.
Her father thought her a genius ; Aunt Polly
was not certain that she was a fool.

It occurred to her that the household was
in ignorance of last night's expedition, and
it was just as well it should not become a
subject for future comment ; so she left the
room hastily and ascended to her chamber.
There she donned her hood and cloak, and,
descending again, went out and crossed the
garden.

It was a queer garden ; such as are found
only upon barren coasts, and had the appearance of much greater age than the house,
which looked very new, despite its proximity
to the sea.   A straight path ran down the
middle, bordered with sea-shells, which were
bleached and chalky ; their crannies filled
with dead weeds.   There was also an attempt
at a wind-brake of stunted cedars, but their
tops were pinched and twisted by the gales
which had swept over them.   An old wall
girting it was patched with bricks like the

house ; the stones, however, were spotted
with lichens, and along the top, repulsive and
inhospitable, was a hardened batter of broken
glass and cement.   It is doubtful if flowers
could have thrived there, even with the persuasion of summer sunshine.

Mercy opened a heavy door in the wall like
that of a fortress and passed out into an obscure road,—obscure in the sense of indefinite-
ness, although glaring and white in the vivid
light.   As smooth as marble, also, for no foot
had trodden it, save her own, since it had
been polished by the friction of the hail blasts
of the previous night.   There were few traces
of vegetation not half-buried in the drifts, and
the sand-hills had changed form so much that,
if the girl had not known her bearings, she
could not have set out at the rapid pace with
which she crossed the marsh ; for there were
great lagoons of sea-water which had risen
with the tide, and lay fringed with dark
green, frost-nipped grass.   Wending her way
between these she reached the O'Doons'
cottage.

It looked smaller than ever.   Only a corner
was left out of the sand which the old man
had no heart to shovel away.   The door stood
open, though neither Mother Margery nor the
fisherman was within.   Mercy suspected they
were searching for driftwood, of which there
was always a great quantity cast up after a
storm.   She ascended the nearest hillock and
cast her eyes along the shore.   Far to the

north two dim figures moved against the white background.

Leaving her cloak in the cabin, for the day was warm, she took instead Mother Margery's shawl. Very pretty she looked as she walked away, although it was hard to tell where the beauty lay. It was of such a character that one yielded to it, won by the magnanimity of her smile, although she seldom smiled. Her name, Mercy, described the grace which modified the impetuosity of her nervous lips, and the intense earnestness of her gray eyes. When she looked at you with her half-absent, lingering gaze, if there were anything unclean in your heart you felt a desire to hide it or to turn away from her. She hated meanness or hypocrisy, and, without knowing it, had the power either of making others afraid of her, or of stimulating the best in them to its noblest effort.

Mercy's feet led her to Mother Margery, but her thoughts were with Jack himself. The hopefulness of youth made her brush a tear away and believe that he would come back. No one had seen him die. Alas! for her he could never die. No man could ever take Jack's place. No peasant could be such a slave, no prince such a benefactor. He was a hero to her, and the courage of his example helped her to meet his aged parents with a smile as they now approached, dragging a sled piled with wood.

It was natural that Mother Margery should

be pulling with steady, undemonstrative
strength, beguiling the old man into thinking
he was no feebler than last year, and that he
was now, as then, bearing the brunt of the
labor himself. That was her way. Mercy
also stepped behind him and laid her hand
on the rope. It was a repetition to her of a
familiar incident, for Jack and she had often
done the same thing.

After the first greeting they walked along
in silence dragging the sled, until Mercy said:
"Aunt Polly is coming down to-day, and I
don't want you to tell her that I was here last
night. If they had known it, I should explain ;
as they do not, it is better as it is."

"You always was that headstrong, it'll be
the death o' you, I'm afeard," said Mother
Margery, doubtfully ; but Mercy had no distrust of her, and they relapsed into silence.

The old man wiped the sweat from his
brow, which showed that he felt the toil as
well as the April sunshine. He sighed, too,
as if with satisfaction. A few years ago he
would have drawn the sled alone, and now he
was a-weary, and so he argued that it would
soon be over and he should follow the seven
sons. Mother Margery looked at him wist-
fully, for she knew the meaning of all his
sighs, and she sighed, too, that he should sigh.

Her strong will and tenacious endurance
could never give up to death while there was
the faintest glimmer of hope or possibility of
any useful thing for her two work-worn hands

to do in the world. The girl understood her
foster-mother, and believed she still hoped for
Jack, while she busied herself with the work
of love before her. She must hold up the old
man's drooping arms and cheer his dying
heart, for he had neither hope nor desire for
it. He knew that hope meant the agony of
winter shipwreck, and he would rather the
boy were dead.

Socially considered, the captain's daughter made a rare choice of friends ; it was
nevertheless the most natural of intimacies,
since our intimates are seldom our equals.
There must be room for influence and expan-
sion. We love best what we admire or com-
miserate. Well-balanced things cannot be
intense, since they lack the pressure which
overcomes scruples and causes devotion. We
love much what we admire and idealize, but
we love more what we pity, sometimes, even,
what we reluctantly despise. For when the
nobler nature makes allowance for the
weaker, and pity takes the place of disdain,
then the heart is full of love. So Mercy
pitied the O'Doons' poverty, their illiterate
uncouthness, and admired, without stint, their
courage and truthfulness and honor.

They admired her, as a being far finer than
themselves, while they pitied her physical
weakness, and this had been since Mother
Margery had sheltered the child at her breast.
And Jack, 'her foster-brother, had helped to
take care of her ; and, mite of a boy though

he was, how valiantly he had carried the baby in his arms through the water to the shore when the tide had caught them in a stranded boat, and she had been so frightened, and clung to him with her arms around his neck.

CHAPTER III.

HEY had not yet reached the cabin when their attention was attracted to a spot far up the beach by the movements of a human figure, which hurried to and fro. Mercy, although expecting her aunt, could not suppose it was she, since, upon closer observation, the figure appeared to be that of a man, accompanied by a three-legged skeleton, with which he was vainly struggling, and which, after a final effort at resistance, fixed its three legs solidly in the sand in a defiant attitude. The singularity of the combination distracted even the O'Doons, and while they paused for a moment to look at it, the skeleton put on a disproportionate breastplate, and the man stepped backward, without taking his eyes off the baleful figure, and stood contemplating it. The party with the sled continued their work, while watching the movements of the other figures.

Suddenly Mercy exclaimed,—

" Why, it must be an artist with one of those folding-easels they carry around."

Even the old man smiled at the grotesqueness of their first impression.

Doubtless curiosity prompted them to quicken their steps, and they soon reached the door of the cabin.

The artist had planted himself on the shelving beach to the southward, and was reconnoitering for a sketch.

Now Mercy, from childhood, had looked upon pictures with admiring wonder ; and as she turned the pages of more than one illustrated magazine, to be found at proper intervals on the table at Blessington House, had wondered how they could have been delineated in so short a time, as the vivid and rapid changes of sea and sky, with which she was familiar, would exact. Here she could have an elucidation of the mystery.

" I'm going to see what he is doing," said she, with the simplicity and decision of one who realized herself mistress of all she surveyed, even to the artist trespassing upon her beach. So, letting go the sled-rope, she set out briskly to investigate him.

It was very plain that the girl was lacking in both the coquetry and scruples which actuate most of her sex, for she walked fearlessly toward the stranger until she was quite close, and then stood and looked at him. I should perhaps say they looked at each other. His smile of surprise and admiration was beyond repression, as he took off his hat as chivalrously as the stiff breeze permitted ; whilst she nodded her head, a little nonplussed, yet having caught the contagion of his smile.

"I am afraid I am trespassing," said he, proceeding to tighten the brass screws of the easel. A wise precaution, else it would have collapsed under the one-sided pressure of the wind.

"Not at all," said Mercy, taking a step nearer, and posing unconsciously, with her head on one side, and her hand on her hip. She was inimitable, and the artist longed to place her, just as she stood. The earnestness of her gray eyes, which she brought to bear upon him, induced him to say what he was thinking. People always told Mercy the truth. Perhaps it was the amount of visible human nature in her, which made one understand that nothing would shock her, unless it were wicked or brutal ; for she anticipated one's wishes to such a surprising degree that one often felt that if he wished to hide his thoughts from her he must hide himself.

She understood at once the young man's eager smile and replied to it :

"I see you would like me to stand just so, as a figure in your picture. I should not mind it, and if it is a very good picture my father would buy it." She thought he was poor and must needs sell his pictures, for his coat was threadbare.

"I do not know how I could ever thank you," replied the artist, much embarrassed.

"Pray do not," said she sententiously.

"But I should be so grateful," said he, still more puzzled, opening his color-box, and looking over his palette. It was in good working order, and he was not slow about beginning. Mercy seemed disposed to be loquacious.

"You do not need to be grateful," she said, smiling. "You are amusing me, and I am obliging you. We are quits."

The artist was working rapidly, but his thoughts were busy as well solving the problem, how a girl, apparently eighteen, speaking good English, dressed in broadcloth, and talking like a philosopher, could possibly exist as one of the fishing folk of Cassandra Bay, and, at the same time, be standing in the surprising relation of a model for himself. He was a bright fellow, but was more at a loss than he had ever been in his life before.

Looking at Mercy, he saw that she was absorbed in herself, and that a look of pain had followed the smile upon her face. He could not solve the enigma, yet he had a dim perception that he was painting at her command, rather than with the exclusive motive of pleasing himself.

First he painted in roughly the red shawl, the dark dress, and the seal-skin hood, blown back by the breeze, so that the oval of her face and head were prettily defined ; but when these had been put in *en masse*, he was forced to say : " I am sorry that you look so sad ; can't you smile the way you did at first ? "

Most persons would have laughed at the idea of being invited to smile, but Mercy only replied, "Do I really look sad?" making an effort to smile which lighted up her helpful eyes with a benignant look, but the smile was very faint. It was a thoughtful face indeed to be imposed upon the world as that of the possible daughter of the hut under the hill. The artist frowned a little, with an unconscious expression of disappointment, but the face had its effect upon him, as it did upon every one. It aroused him to his noblest effort, and he put it in truly, with such a sincerity in the gaze of the eyes, that they were as Mercy's own.

"There! I shall not touch it again, for fear I overwork it. Will you look at it?" said he, after a moment, stepping back that she might come and see it.

"Oh, how very pretty!" cried the girl, with unfeigned delight. "I should not have thought I was half as pretty as that. My father will be so pleased with it. Some day you will bring it to the house and show it to him?"

This was said inquiringly, but authoritatively as well.

The figure, although so small, had taken up more time than either Mercy or the artist had realized. He had been unconscious of the flight of time because interested in his work, and she, having lapsed into one of her brown studies, had been equally oblivious. He now took the opportunity of scrutinizing her face.

"I should be glad to think I was like that," she said earnestly, "and it will look very picturesque with Mother Margery's cottage in the distance on one side, and the wide green sea on the other, and those ragged sand cliffs to help out the foreground. I have often thought I should like to paint. Does it take long to learn?"

"That depends," said he slowly. "They say 'geniuses are plodders,' and that adage probably grows out of the fact that those who love anything fervently are apt to give their time, and strength, and patience toward doing it well." The spirit of this reply was evident in the work before her, which showed the finish and facility of a devoted hand.

Just at that moment, lifting her eyes, Mercy caught sight of Aunt Polly fluttering across the dunes. Her figure was unmistakable, for she despised the meanness of the present style and still sported the full skirts and round waists of twenty years ago; and the breeze was spreading, like wide wings, the albatross-gray breadths of her gown, as she swooped down from the sand-hills upon the helpless cot of the O'Doons.

"I must go!" exclaimed Mercy suddenly, "for I see Aunt Polly coming over the hill."

Without farther explanation, she walked off in the direction of the cabin, somewhat vainglorious at having had her portrait so flatteringly painted, for she never doubted her future possession of it. Had she been older, there

would also have mingled with her feelings a
pleasant satisfaction in knowing there was
being preserved something of the freshness
and picturesqueness of her youth. The artist
looked after her rather dazed.

"Well! That is an episode!" he exclaimed aloud, laughing to himself. "By Jove!
It's enormous." The adjective referred to
the success of the sketch. "Immense!" he
continued, muttering from time to time, as
he walked back and forth, to estimate the
values of the sea and sand he was introduc-
ing as accessories. "Wants me to show it
to papa, does she! And what might papa
say if he knew that his strong-minded daughter, with gushing simplicity, had been posing
for a vagabond artist, like yours humbly,
Algernon Abercrombie—otherwise Algie, and
sometimes at small pay, as A A. Roman capi-
tals in monogram." There was a touch of
satire in the young man's voice as he drew
the monogram in the sand with the end of
a reed cane he had used for a mahl-stick.
"And what'll 'Old Arthur' have to say for
you, my pretty sea-maiden?" continued he,
after an industrious interval. "Old Arthur"
was the studio-name of a well-known marine
painter of his acquaintance. "By Jove, what
a catch! As good fish in the sea as ever
came out! I always said so!"

He picked up a stubby stick, and, unfolding
it into an uncomfortable three-legged stool,
walked off with it, and shoved it into the sand

at a good and sufficient distance ; and, settling himself upon it, lighted a cigarette and
proceeded to gaze admiringly at the picture,
which was beyond dispute one of those rare
successes of open-air effect, which, being
painted under a vivid impression of the scene,
make an appealing success. "Won't they
smile, when she grows a little larger!" he
continued, flourishing the cane vaguely to
express a vast enlargement of the canvas ;
and, having finished his cigarette, he fell to
whistling "Beautiful Isle of the Sea," to the
accompaniment of various admiring attitudes
and exclamations. "And fair are the smiles
of thy daughters."

Meantime Mercy, oblivious of the comedy
he was performing solo, sat in a corner of the
O'Doons' cabin, wrapped in frowning silence.
Aunt Polly was holding forth, after having
read aloud various tracts ; old O'Doon submitting passively, as devoid of resistance as
of emotion, for the energy of the man was
gone from within him, and it is hardly possible to think he could have been aroused,
even to the interest of saving his own soul.

When she paused, the lull of the silence recalled him, as any change will upon occasion,
and he replied drily : "I don't dispute ez the
man war a-tellin' the truth ez fur ez his experience tuk him, but my opinion allus war
that it ain't no use a-takin' a man's convictions
fur evidence, whar they ain't give in cole blood.
When a man's a-dyin' o' shipwreck, or any-

thin' else, he'll promise the good Lord any-
thin' he's a mind to ; but it ain't no use be-
lievin' him, tell you sees how he gits along
when he's prosp'rous. Prosperity's bin the
devil ter catch many a poor man's soul afore
to-day. Now that's one thing I allus admired 'bout'n my boy Jack. He tuk luck
with a pow'ful steady head ; en my 'pinion is
that them's the sort what's born to a savin'
grace."

This speech was utterly heterodox to Aunt
Polly, who listened with an expression of disgust modified with commiseration.

"Surely you can't believe that your boy
John was born to go to heaven without a creed,
and without even being baptized, or so much
as repenting of his sins ?" said Aunt Polly
aghast.

"Jack allus war that good, marm. I've tole
his mother afore to-day, that he war too good
to live ; " said the old man with conviction.

Aunt Polly looked at him with a dogmatic
glitter in her pale blue eyes.

"Madam," said O'Doon humbly, "I ain't a-
speakin' fur myself. I ain't got no goodness
ter speak on, leastways none in partic'lar.
I war a-speakin' fur Jack," he added apologetically. The pathetic leaving of himself entirely outside of all personal claim of merit
reminded Mercy of the contrast between the
Pharisee and the Publican ; but she managed
to restrain herself from interfering, and looked
at her aunt, awaiting her reply.

Now, if sincerity atones for unfortunate results, Aunt Polly's good intentions deserve the shelter of a very broad mantle of charity.

" But don't you think that at your age it's time you *were* talking about yourself? " replied Aunt Polly.

" I can't say ez how I see any particular good in it, marm," replied O'Doon, with doubt and indifference.

" It is not only good, but it is necessary," cried the lady, edging her chair closer to his, and adding, with ecclesiastical severity, " except ye believe, ye shall *all* likewise perish."

" Believe what ? "

Aunt Polly paused ere she replied. At length she said, " That our Lord Jesus Christ came into the world to save sinners, *of whom you are the chief.*"

" Well, I don't know about subscribin' to that offhan', fur there's been times when I've seed men what I had my doubts about bein' *wusuner.* There ain't nuthin, marm, like a little honest considerashun afore subscribin' to sich like. There ain't no use fur a man to set a less 'pinion on hisself than he's got. It allus 'peared to me to be lackin' in self-respec'. I ain't never killed nobody, leastways not ez I knows on ; I ain't never stole, *never* ; en I ain't had much 'casion ter lie to nobody, fur lyin' is mostways the fruits of bein' afeared ; an' I can't say ez how I'm much afeared, 'ceptin' o' the sea, and there ain't no use o' lyin' to the sea, fur it won't do no good ; nor

to the Lord neither, he's sort o' apt to fin' us
out ; so I reckon I ain't a mind to subscribe
to them sentiments, marm."

After a pause the old man added: "I ain't
a-makin' no comments on nobody else's religion, but all the same I sort o' feel ez ef I
would be some sort o' a hypercrite ef I set up
ter be better'n I be."

Aunt Polly heaved a disappointed sigh.
Clearly she must shift her tack, if she hoped
to approach the barren land of O'Doon's sterile
imagination. She looked blankly before her,
as if she were considering the possibilities of
the case, and then arose, and bade the O'Doons
good-bye, saying to the old man, as she shook
hands with him, "I hope you will give this little
talk some serious consideration," and then,
—it was her way,—having administered her
admonition, she took a blue flannel shirt out
of a hand-basket and gave it to him and de-
parted. The kindness of the act, being an
expression of good feeling and sympathy, probably did more to impress her homily than any
of the tracts she had applied with unction.
The generosity of a silent example would have
done more and not have aroused the resistance of argument.

However, he looked at the shirt critically,
felt the thickness of the flannel, and, after letting it lie on his knee for a while, gave it to
Mother Margery to put away in the white
cupboard.

Mercy was still sitting by the fire ; not hav-

ing accompanied her aunt. It mattered very
little, for the O'Doons' cottage stood as a kind
of outpost between Blessington House and the
sea, and the girl was subject to erratic wan-
derings between the two.

"Sometimes I don't know whether I've got
any religion or not," said Mercy, in a tone of
uncertainty. "I don't think I quite like the
idea of talking love to God; but I *believe* a
good deal."

"Well, I don't know ez I believe very
much," said O'Doon, looking at the fire, "but
I ain't got no notion o' tryin' to fool the good
Lord with no sort o' humbug. Not ez I mean
ter p'int the idee that your Aunt Polly is the
like o' that; but them's my notions all the
same. But I respec's other folks's sentiments," he added politely, casting his eye
toward the blue shirt.

"Well, my notion," spoke up Mother
Margery, who entered into the argument for
the first time, "my notion is, that some folks
talks, it's natur' to 'em, and some folks *believes*,
without talkin' much; and some folks *works*.
Jes' does what they finds to do and don't
make no fuss about it. And some folks is got
a mixture o' all sorts. Jes' accordin' to the
natur' of 'em; an' every one of us, when we're
sort o' took by surprise, is apt to do something
different from what we ever 'spected o' ourselves. I've done things afore to-day that
was that good they's surprised myself!"

This was such a long speech for Mother

Margery that her listeners looked at her in wonder.

The memory of many noble acts stirred in the old man's mind, and he replied with a rough chivalry that touched Mercy to the heart, "Well, it ain't surprised nobody else, I'll be bound!"

CHAPTER IV.

HE scene had changed with the fall of the tide. The mirror-like pools were gone from the marshes, and Mercy followed a dank foot-path which meandered uninvitingly through them.

Her life, hitherto monotonous, had suddenly become thrilling ; and she lived from day to day in a fever of anxiety.

When with others, she resolutely resisted their depression, endeavoring to encourage them as well ; but when alone, a sickening dread made her heart sink.

Upon entering the house her presence was acknowledged by a subdued rattling of chairs, and after a short interval a little dark man came in at the door, and crossed the padded carpet to a dumb-waiter beside the chimney. Very quietly and quickly he moved in his list slippers, and after a few moments Aunt Polly and Mercy sat down at the table.

It would take a long time to tell the history of each inmate of the Captain's house ; though they were all people with histories, accessory to the central figure, whom all hated, feared, loved, would even have died for, so violent and contrary were his characteristics.

The Captain was a man at once fickle and steadfast. When he gave way to his ungovernable temper, as he often did, it was with the overpowering fury of the moment; an hour later he would go to the ends of the earth to make amends. Beneath it was a solid rock of steadfast prejudice which nothing could unsettle. Casual acquaintances often feared or hated him, knowing only the surface of the man; but the helpless or poor, who sought shelter in his strength, loved him so they would have died for him, if need be.

His "curios," as those who hated him called the collection of beast, bird, and humankind which inhabited Blessington House, were extraordinary, and had been picked up and brought hither from Heaven knows where.

There was Antonio, who was said to have come with Columbus, and who looked like a mummy, stoop-shouldered and bandy-legged. He had figured in many high travesties at Blessington House, when the Captain wrought himself to fury and repented again with farcical suddenness and contrition.

Antonio, having sailed the wide seas as steward of the Captain's brig, in the natural order of things had settled down on shore with him when luck and oysters had made the master rich. He was a Roman Catholic, whom Aunt Polly had vainly endeavored to convert from the sin and folly of his idolatry. But her fervor had slowly subsided, and she

had concluded that his devotion must indeed
be perfunctory, since he held to worshipping a
storm-battered image of the " Blessed Lady,"
and a crucifix without arms and with a
broken nose.   There was a pathetic history
pertaining to these strange idols, which her
Episcopalian orthodoxy could never have
understood, although Mercy and the Captain
ever treated the little mystery with a lenient
respect ; for they saw that, in the poetic fancy
of the Italian, each had a meaning.   He, also,
was one of Mercy's phenomenal coadjutors
and humble friends.   Whatever she thought,
wished, or said, he swore by, with unquestion-
ing faith and a tropical ardor which neither
age nor climate had cooled.

That morning, having served the omelette
and broiled ham, he had just settled himself
for support against the back of her chair
(which act, of late years, had showed infirmity), when there were demonstrations of impatience at the door.   "Antonio, do let Sailor
come in ! " exclaimed Mercy, looking around.
Antonio did as he was bid, and immediately,
when the door was opened, in rushed a
hideous dog, whisking his tail and bounding
from one lady to the other.

" Oh, you dreadful creature, do get away ! "
cried Aunt Polly, flinging up her arms.   " He
never will learn that I can't endure a dog,
never ! "

Now Aunt Polly had made this speech
every day since she had first come to Bless-

ington House, ten years or more ago.
"Sailor" was a veteran, an Irish poodle, of
the brownest, kinkiest, most yellow-eyed
variety, and was as jolly an old tar as ever a
dog could be. He was devoted to his master,
but with such inconstancy that, in the absence
of the master, he was satisfied with his master's daughter. He sat on his haunches, with
his head as high as the table, and ate small
scraps of bread and butter which Mercy
placed on his nose, and which, with rickety
wistfulness, he tossed, and caught occasionally in his mouth. Perhaps this trick vexed
him ; at any rate he barked so vehemently at
last that Mercy sent Antonio for a bone.

There were two other of the Captain's odd-
ities below. "Below" meant the kitchen, for
the house was run like a ship ashore, and
things went by nautical names.

Bill Junk was the cook, and had a voice
like thunder, and sang sea-songs and love-
ditties when not otherwise engaged. At other
times he could be heard humming, humming,
as monotonously as the sea itself.

Luncheon was a silent affair, and when it
was finished Mercy and her aunt returned to
the fireside. Aunt Polly's arm moved monotonously as she stitched upon another blue
shirt, and her mind was equally busy com-
posing homilies. Mercy was knitting. It
would be difficult to tell how many comforters
she knit, as, hour by hour, through the long
winter days, her ivory needles moved in and

out, while her thoughts wandered about the world.

At half-past six there was a commotion below. The great gate had opened and shut, and a heavy tread had sounded upon the shell drive. Mercy ran to the window. She heard her father's voice shouting : " Hold her steady ! "

Any locomotive animal was *her* in the Captain's vocabulary, so that there was no incongruity to him in applying that pronoun to the large and heavy-stepping Percheron gelding which, too fat for its own comfort, was kept to transport the gig across the sands to the nearest station.

When the master arrived, every one must needs know it. He was not secretive. He despised secrecy, as he thought he hated the devil, and was forever talking about both. Mercy heard him saying, " What the devil are you fellows about, that you can't never be a-lookin' out fur me when I come home. Here ! I've been two mortal hours a-crossin' them cussed sands in the cold, till my fingers is nigh onto froze, an' won't none o' you take the trouble to see I've got my gloves to start with, en you—all o' you with nuthin' to do but warm yer lazy shins afore the fire. 'Fore the Lord, I'll be damned if I ain't wore out with no sort of attention ! "

The large horse, with Italian appreciation of the feminine pronoun, neighed with satisfaction as he turned his head toward the

stable, nearly whisking Splugen out of the
gig with a sweep of his long tail ; while the
Captain, blowing like a monsoon, entered the
house and swaggered upstairs.

" Well, Mercy," said he, " you see me !
I've got back, and I ain't got no news neither,
an' I wish ter the Lord you'd teach them boys
some sort o' manners, fur they ain't got none.
Here, pull off them shoes o' mine ! I must be
gittin' the rheumatiz ! It's nothin' but this
damned frosty air what's a-ruinin' my consti-
tution. If it wa'n't that I'm sort o' comfortable here, I'd clear out ! I allus knowed that
no man but jus' such a idjut ez me would
put a sight o' money in a pile o' brick whar the
wind's that bleak the runtiest ole pitch pine
dasn't grow high enough to hide nothin'. I
used ter tell yer ma that, but she war that tied
down to these here sand-hills that she couldn't
b'lieve nothing tell she caught her death o'
cole, en 'twas too late ! "

The Captain's breath being exhausted, his
thoughts wandered in silence to the sodless,
wind-swept graveyard, where only wild vines
ventured, creeping like criminals.

" Your toes *are* cold ! " said Mercy sympathetically, taking her father's slippers off
again and feeling the ends of his socks.

" Cold ! " exclaimed the Captain, as if she
had doubted his veracity, " I should think
they was cold. Damned cold ! "

Those who have no knowledge of Scandi-
navian mythology and its purgatorial regions

rifted with hail-blasted gulches of perpetual ice may not be able to understand how his feet were damned and cold at once. Such, however, by the will of Odin, is possible.

However, we must take the rough old skipper as we find him, without marginal notes, and judge him only by his intentions and actions, which were usually generous if vehement.

Mercy sat down on the floor and took possession of her father's extremities as if they had been two brawny babies, and proceeded to rub them. The Captain thawed under sympathy and devoured it like pap, so that in a few moments the warmth of the fire after the breezy drive, the luxurious softness of the cushioned chair, and the gentle rubbing which had wittingly diminished to a very comforting and drowsy titillation, caused him to forget his good behavior and fall asleep.

He slept with such satisfaction, that Mercy enjoyed it out of sympathy, although it was of that quality of repose which is punctuated by blasts both loud and shrill, echoing from wall to wall, like the blare of a bugle.

This great rough monster, for so he might be considered if transported into the midst of a tea-party of fashionable women, was something about as guileless as a high-tempered, frolicksome, good-natured, generous and repentant baby would be,—looked at through a magnifying-glass, and spiritually enlarged as well.'

Mercy knew her father like a book; she could as freely open his heart and read it; and, when she was satisfied with the result of her manipulation, she arose from the floor, and, settling herself comfortably in a chair, resumed her knitting.

Aunt Polly having retired to her room, Mercy spent half an hour alone with her unconscious parent, until a snore too great for utterance awoke the Captain with a shudder. After looking around, rubbing his eyes, and yawning, the surprised exclamation escaped him, " Why, I must ha' been asleep ! "

" Yes," said Mercy, " it *sounded* so. You forget walls have ears ! Do you know I had the funniest time to-day."

" How's that ? " inquired the Captain, wide awake at once, with his mind quite refreshed.

" Why, I had my portrait painted."

" By Jiminy ! " The Captain was awake in earnest. " Who the devil's been here ? "

" Nobody's been here; I've been somewhere."

Now there's no curiosity equal to that of a big, blustering, good-natured man, who professes to despise the failings of the weaker sex.

" Where have you been ? "

" Down to Mother Margery's."

" Down to Mother Margery's to have your portrait painted ! You may tell that to the marines, an' give 'em my love."

"Oh, he wouldn't want your love, he's a handsome young man."

"A handsome young man, painting portraits at Mother Margery's ! What the devil do you mean ? "

"I mean what I say. I went to Mother Margery's ; a handsome young man was there ; I walked up to him, and he looked at me, and then he painted my portrait, and I said, 'Thank 'e, sir,' like any good girl, and came away."

"Some ragged vagabond peddling signboards for a living, I'll be bound,"—with disgust.

"Yes," doubtfully from Mercy, "made a good one of me, and I thought 'twould suit you for your shop," indicating, with a nod, the other side of the house ; "and so I said to him, 'fetch it along,' and perhaps he will."

"What in creation did you do that for ? "

"So you'd have a portrait of me when you and Aunt Polly send me away to be a fine lady." This last in rather a quavering voice.

The father bristled at once. "Who said I was goin' to send you away ? "

"Well, you just needn't, I can tell you, for I'll come home, if I have to walk ; and you can buy the young man's picture too. It's beautiful, and just like me, and I want it."

"Sounds like it. What's your young man's name ? "

"I'm sure I don't know. He's very well behaved, and he's got red hair."

" Red hair ! Good Lord ! " with an expression of disgust. " You may tell him to send along his pictur', and stay at home hisself. Damn a fellow with red hair ! "

" Oh, he's quite lovely, I assure you," said Mercy with an enigmatical smile.

"Some little jackanapes from Richmond I'll be bound, dead-beat I bet, to be huntin' a livin' at Cassandra Bay, less'n he can live off'n clams and seaweed."

" I think he may be poor enough. Indeed I don't doubt it, for his coat was threadbare."

" Hungry did ye say ? " with a manner at once softened.

" He might be," said Mercy slyly.

" Why didn't you bring him up ? Bring him up by all means, and give him something to eat."

" How could I when he's got red hair ? "

" We can't allow a man to starve outside our very gate ! " cried the Captain excitedly, with an oratorical gesture. " Look out and see if he is there ! "

" Why, father, how you let your imagination run away with you ! It's pitch-dark out of doors. He was a real gentleman, with the most elegant manners and a threadbare coat."

" Painting sign-posts for a living ! " interrupted the Captain, chuckling contemptuously.

" Now, listen to me ; I said he painted *me ;* I'm not a post."

" No ; but let me hear about it."

4

"Well, this was the way. Old Ned and Mother Margery were dragging driftwood on the beach——"

"There it is again," interrupted the Captain, "I told them confounded old fools to let the wood alone, and I'd have it draw'd for 'em!"

"Well, all the same, they were hauling on the old sled, and I went to help haul too."

"By Jiminy, hear that!"

"And when we got to the door, I saw a man on the beach with the funniest easel, and I made it my business to see what he was up to. When I got nearly to him I found he was painting a picture of Mother Margery's cottage and the sea; and I knew by the way he looked at me that he wanted to put me in it."

"Damned familiar."

"Why, no; I thought it was splendid, and I told him so. So he painted me in, and it's beautiful!"

"Humph!" Long silence, broken by Mercy, persuasively,—

"And I knew that you would like a nice picture of me, and so I told him to be sure and bring it here for you to buy."

"Who pays for all the things we buy, you or me?"

"I could if you'd give me the money."

"Yes, there's no doubt you could." This was said in a tone intended to be sarcastic; but satire was not the Captain's forte, so he

relapsed into what he wished should be inter-
preted as surly silence ; but even that was so
easily misunderstood that Mercy said quite
cajolingly : "Say, now, you will buy it, won't
you ? Promise me you will, and "—thoughtfully—" I'll tell you what I'll do. I'll tickle
your toes till you go to sleep for a week."

"I don't want to go to sleep for a week. I
ain't dead !"

"I meant every afternoon for a week, till
you go to sleep."

The Captain looked at his slippers reflectively. When he paused to consider, he
paused to yield ; and when he yielded, it was
not in miniature.

"How big is the pictur' ? "

"About so big," indicating sixteen by
twenty inches.

"Now, what does you s'pose, at my time
o'life, I wants with such a damn little scrap
as that ? Do you think I wants to be a puttin'
on specticles every time I look at a pictur'
o' you ? Fetch him along ; 'long as you will
have it, I know there ain't no peace fur me
till I gives in to you, and while you're 'bout it
tell him to put up somethin' handsome, and
damned handsome too ! None o' yer pewter
platters for me ! "

The Captain considered that he had an apt
mind for comparison.

A retort was ready upon Mercy's lips, when
the door was quietly opened, and Aunt Polly,
a stickler for propriety, entered, dressed for

dinner in an old-fashioned tabby silk, with the lustre and cut of a quarter of a century ago.

Mercy, knowing it was late, hastened to her room. The Captain rang the bell, and Antonio carried out a programme which had not been altered in his memory of Blessington House.

"Fetch her out, Tony," said the Captain affectionately; he could not realize that the old steward had arrived at the dignity of Antonio. Surely he did not look like a mummy to his master. Antonio promptly glided across to the old mahogany cupboard and brought thence a decanter of gin and four large tumblers, which the Captain placed in a row beside his own plate upon the table, already laid. He then filled the glasses, each in turn, half full from the decanter, and, with a smile of the most cordial hospitality, waved his hand to three imaginary *bons camarades*, drank his own down, fiery and undiluted, with the exclamation, "Let her go!" as if he were dropping an imaginary anchor in an imaginary haven of rest. Antonio waited until the skipper had finished his performance, and then, with a profound bow, disappeared with the four glasses, three of which were yet untasted; and a moment later, with a strange imitation of the master's manner and cordial smile, the three *bons camarades* down below waved their glasses and cried, "Here's luck to her!" meaning the roof over them, and all under it, and drank, as the master had done, the undiluted liquor.

Then Antonio, thus enlivened, hurried the hot dishes into the dumb-waiter, sent it whiz-zing upward by a twitch of his elbow, and pattered after it with his slippered feet. "They sends obedience, sir," said he, proceeding to arrange the dinner.

Mercy returned in a few moments, looking very sad. When she was not cajoling her father she seemed to have no power to force a smile to her face. Her heart was heavy, but she was studiously alert to hide it. The conversation at dinner was spasmodic, and, as soon afterward as it was possible, she stole off to bed ; but once within the seclusion of her own room, with the door locked behind her, the girl threw aside the deception as a masker his mask, and, sinking down upon the rug before the fire, abandoned herself to an exhausting outpour of bitter tears and imploring prayers for Jack.

CHAPTER V

T an early hour the next morning— and the same will hold good, with rare exception, of every morning of the year—the Captain's door was heard to bang, and his voice, more or less interrupted by a muscular struggle, heard shouting, as if to a watch aloft :

"Mercy, Mercy, git up!" Another almost suffocating effort : "Git up, it's high time you was up! Sleepin' away the whole day, and leavin' yer poor ole daddy with nobody to talk to, instead o' gettin' up betimes and seein' as there's some sort o' breakfus' ready fur a hungry man to eat!"

His ejaculations became more muttered as he interested himself in his performances.

The truth is, the Captain always awoke in a bad humor, and with an oppressive sense of loneliness ; for he was excessively communicative, and as soon as he was wide awake he wanted some one to talk to, and no one suited him as well as Mercy.

As for the poor child, she only turned uneasily upon her pillow and fell asleep again.

Now, each morning, no matter where the

thermometer ranged, it was the Captain's custom to have a good *swab off*, probably considering that his broad chest bore some resemblance to the deck of a ship. After that, when sufficiently arrayed, he would fling his door open and bang it after him.

Finding his shoes ready outside, he would thrust his feet into them and begin panting and lacing up and shouting for Mercy, all in a breath—swearing vehemently at the shoe-tackle which exasperated him.

Having accomplished tying his shoes, he would stand upright and shake himself to settle his trousers, struggling into the loops of his suspenders, which had hitherto been festooned about him. Then he would fling on his waistcoat, which, with his watch—which was a steady old machine and defied corruption from bad treatment—in the pocket, had hung on the door-knob all night.

As soon as he had elbowed himself into his coat he considered his toilet complete, and descended the stairs.

"Get down!" angrily to Sailor, who met him joyfully at the foot of the stairs, and could not learn that his master always got up as cross as a bear. "There ain't room enough in this house yet. Positively I can't set my foot down without stepping on a dog!" Still, he managed to find his way to the back door, which he unbolted and flung open, letting in a shivering draft of wind and fog. Looking around, peering into the mist, he presently discerned a dark object, which proved to be Bill Junk, returning from the ash-pile with an empty cinder-box.

"I say, man, spread out the mainsail, en turn her about, it's time we was done breakfast long ago ! Lyin' in bed till the mornin's half gone. Send up Tony, and be damned quick too ; I ain't got no use fur sich a lazy crew !" With this he was sufficiently chilled to relish the dining-room fire ; so he slammed to the door, and, jerking out the big silver watch by a chain as stout as a dog-collar, retired, muttering objurgations between his teeth throughout which the fact of the hour being six figured conspicuously. Then he settled himself in his arm-chair and took a nap, while Antonio noiselessly crept in and laid the table. Inconsistency, thy name is Solomon Blessington !

He was insensible to Aunt Polly's matutinal greeting, and had to be spoken to with emphasis when breakfast, in reasonable time, had been served.

Before he sat down, the ceremony of "grog" was repeated, and then the Captain and Aunt Polly proceeded with their meal. But before helping himself, or allowing anyone else to be helped, he took the carving knife and fork and felt all over the beefsteak ; and when he had decided, by that process, which was the tenderest spot, he cut that part out carefully and transferred it to a plate which Antonio held ready, spread a spoonful of dish-gravy over it, and bade him "keep it hot." The old man placed it in the dumb-waiter and consigned it to Bill Junk. Aunt Polly, prompt and punctual, remembering the deserts of the early bird, for ten years had had cause to resent this partiality, and habitu-ally straightened her lips with indignation ; but it was lost on the Captain, and equally so on the object of the little attention, who was still asleep upstairs.

He was now ready to proceed with break-fast in earnest. He gave Aunt Polly the best of all that remained, which might have satis-fied her had she not had an inordinate sense of her own dignity, and could she have realized the moral of the fact that he was content with what might have been considered the scraps, for himself.

In about two hours Mercy appeared and gave her father a loving greeting, which he accepted with a grunt.

The fog had lifted and there was a clear prospect for the day.

After ringing for Antonio, Mercy went to the window and looked out. Far away, be-yond the garden wall, stretched countless rolling sand-hills, and on the summit of one of them was the painter with his easel.

"There he goes!" cried Mercy excitedly, laughing so immoderately that the tears came into her eyes. Her father's curiosity being aroused, he came and stood beside her at the window.

" Who goes ? I don't sec nothin'."

" Why, the painter and his easel. Look over there ; the wind has blown them both down and is spoiling his picture with the sand."

" A redic'lus fool ! To expec' to stan' up agin the north win' with them rickety sticks and no sort o' stanchions."

" Let's go out and see him," said Mercy. " But wait a minute for me, till I've finished my breakfast,"—beginning to eat it in a great hurry.

The Captain meanwhile stood watching the other man, muttering to himself, " Deserves to blow down ! Any cussid fool what'll stan' right squar' in front o' a solid house and not make no efforts to git inside an' work, the same as me, a-lookin' out'n the window, don't have no right to succeed."

Being uncommonly fond of giving advice, he was not reluctant to accompany Mercy when she had put on her cloak and hood, but strode after her, attended by Sailor, who ran ahead, wagging his grisly old stump of a tail, upon which the brown hair kinked in knotty little curls like cockle-burrs.

It was rather cold, and the Captain thrust his hands in his pockets to keep them warm, as he marched along with a reminder of the sailor's roll in his walk, although he had acquired, with his increasing corpulency, something of the rich man's swagger. He wore a broad-brimmed black silk hat, considerably wind-shaken and shaggy, which, with his spacious trousers, cut with sailor's breadth of style, gave him altogether a portly and imposing appearance, and there was an assurance of authority in his double-breasted broadcloth coat notwithstanding that it glistened along the seams.

Mercy, buttoned up to the ears in sealskin, followed him. When the Captain arrived within shouting distance he began : "'Pears to me you might a-chose a better place to be a-tumblin' aroun'! It's a frosty mornin' to sport yerse'f like a weather-cock, afore ye fin' out that the gale's a-blowin' three p'ints to east o' north. I say, stranger, I dunno yer name, you'd better come over and warm up a bit."

The artist looked at him in astonishment. He had been so interested in his own exploits, that he had not observed the approach of the party.

"Oh," he gasped, proceeding to pack the dry sand around the unstable easel.

The Captain, accustomed to pouring forth advice in unmeasured quantities upon the humble folk about him, expected all others to receive it with equal avidity, and was indignant and disappointed if they did not.

"Thank you very much," said the stranger graciously, pausing for breath, "but I have only a few days to spare and I must make the most of them. I seem to have made a mess of it thus far, however." Suddenly catching sight of Mercy, he blushed crimson, with that excessive sensitiveness peculiar to persons with hair of a golden red.

"Well, I don't see no sense in this sort o' thing at all. What's it you are tryin' ter git ?" inquired the Captain, floundering up the steep side of the sand-hill, and getting very red and angry, with his shoe-tops full of grit, against which the vaunting breadth of his trousers offered no protection. "I can't see ez you 'pears to be accomplishin' much o' nothin'," he volunteered, when he had reached the top, wind-broken and red, shoving his hat back to get a better view of what the young man was about. The faint blear of blue sky in the picture was smudged with sand, and the artist looked crestfallen and disconsolate.

"I say, Mercy, is this here your young man ?" inquired the Captain, suddenly recollecting the agreement which had been perpetrated over night.

"Yes, he's the one," said Mercy, smiling a little at the absurdity of the question, and at what the "young man" must think of it.

"Has you got yer pictur' along ?" asked the skipper, turning to the artist, who was suffering another relapse of blushes.

The Captain could not conceive what he was blushing about, and stared vainly at his pockets, expecting to see the picture sprouting out of one of them.

Algernon Abercrombie, artist and gentleman, looked in bewilderment from one to the

other and at Sailor, who, with a genuine touch
of masculine curiosity, had begun to mix mat-
ters still farther by tramping in the color-box
and bursting the tubes of paint.

"I don't see no portrait," said the Captain
blankly, turning to Mercy with an injured expression. "How's that, young man? By the
by, what's your name?"

"Abercrombie," replied Algernon.

"Well, Mr. Aber—Aber—Aber*corn*, jes'
fetch 'em along, an' we'll find some sort o' snug-
ger port than this here," replied the Captain,
making a face at the bleak wind, and speaking
as one having authority. "I ain't got no use fur
no sich," glancing around with large contempt;
"there ain't nothin' like solid comfort; nothin'
like sittin' down behin' a wall when the win'
blows. I'm a man o' solid notions, sir! Did
ye ever have the rheumatiz? Well, we'll all on
us have it, if you don't hurry; an' the nex' time
you happens along here, jes' step in, and don't
stop to ax no questions. The mos' I hates,
is folks what's a-holdin' off all the time. Yes,
come on along o' us; you won't be the fust
stranger, an' I 'lows you ain't a-goin' to be the
las', what's drunk a dram with Sol Blessin'-
ton; 'less'n the mainsheet breaks, en I ain't a-
hearken to it. Come along with ye! I ain't
got no objection to helpin' ye myse'f," said
the Captain, suiting the action to the word,
and, without further parley, uprooting the
easel and starting down the sand-hill with it.
But he had not proceeded far when the sand

gave way beneath his feet and he flung the slight structure far into the air in his vain endeavor to right himself. He failed in that attempt ; and both the artist and Mercy, notwithstanding their efforts to the contrary, shook with suppressed laughter at sight of him, as, with widespread arms, and legs vainly clawing the loose sand which followed him in showers, he slid down the hillock. "If he hadn't a-been such a darned fool, none o' this wouldn't a-happened," cried the Captain, struggling to his feet and endeavoring to spit the sand out of his mouth, breathless with anger and embarrassment.

"No," said Mercy sympathetically, "if you hadn't been so kind trying to help him and make him more comfortable, you could have looked out for yourself better."

"It's jes' the way with them idjuts, always a-tryin' ter do things without no sort o' reason about the wind or the weather, an' jes' see what it's come to!"

"Oh, you'll soon be all right, you're cold. Let's go home. I'll carry the canvas and you carry the easel, and he'll be sure to follow." So she picked them up from where they had fallen, and, giving her father the easel, retained the canvas herself.

Meanwhile Algernon, standing on the summit of the sand-hill, was enjoying the *contretemps* immensely, fully realizing that "a hearty laugh is often the best introduction," and making a very sound estimate of the char-

acters and relations of his new acquaintances.
He shut up his paint-box and followed them.

As they walked along, the Captain was too
disgusted for words, and Mercy much too
wise, while Mr. Abercrombie submitted without resistance to the fate which was dragging
him, "will he nil he" into the great brick
house, looking for all the world like a county
jail, with its heavy, nail-studded gate set in the
moss-grown wall coped with battered glass
and cement. Still, the childlike overgrown
simplicity of the skipper, and the earnestness
of his daughter, who appeared to be a chip
out of the very heart of the old block, made
the young artist yield himself, without reserve,
to these powers that be. Even Sailor had an
uncommon ugliness which appealed to human
sympathy at large.

Algernon felt a sense of protection when the
oaken shutters swung to after them, and in-
cluded him within their fold ; and an undi-
vided curiosity possessed him as he looked
around at the stunted wind-break, the chalky
shell borders, and doubtful flower-beds before
the door.

Antonio, Bill Junk, and Splugen, accompanied by the inevitable green parrot, peep-
ing out of the mess-room window, with their
heads in a line, seeing their master and mistress so unusually laden, came out, eager to
relieve them.

"Here you are, one and all !" roared the
Captain, as glad of a chance to bellow as

a bull with a bee-sting. "I'll be bound fur it, got nothin' to do but to be a-investigatin' everything ye see ! I suppose you'd all like this here gentleman to think we ain't never seen a artist before !"

Out of the very fullness of the heart the mouth sometimes speaketh, and it is not to be doubted that this was the first time a person in that line of accomplishment had crossed the threshold of Blessington House. But hospitality speedily changed his temper, and turning to Algernon with a sudden bland smile the Captain exclaimed, "Come in, sir, come in, it's agreeable !" waving his hand majestically, so that no doubt was left in Algie's mind as he entered the deep-set and massive portal, the open door of which Antonio was holding in his hand ready to close after them.

"Hurry up, Bill Junk, and let's have tea !" cried a harsh voice in the dark corridor, which sounded so supernatural and uncanny that it made Algie start. "It's that damned bird ; jest don't make yourself oneasy," said the Captain apologetically, leading the way up the stairs to the dining-room, and almost languid with affability.

When the Captain had himself chosen a chair for Algie and induced him to occupy it,— for in his own house he was as polite as a mandarin,—he rang for Antonio.

"Fetch her out, Tony !" he cried, with his hospitable smile and a gracious wave in the direction of the cupboard, and Tony produced the decanter and glasses, adding one for the stranger. The Captain poured out his usual half tumbler, apologizing for not making it stronger, and then offered the decanter to the young man, who looked at it with a little uncertainty.

"It's mild, sir, mild as milk !" said the Captain impatiently, holding his glass already half-way to his lips. "Howsomesever, I ain't pressin' ; suit yer own convenience, Mr.—Mr. Applecorn—I clean forgits yer name."

"Abercrombie," suggested Algie, pouring out a shallow quantity into the bottom of his tumbler and looking around vainly for a jug of water.

"Water !" exclaimed the Captain. "Pshaw, man, that ain't no mor'n a shadder. Tony, fetch him the water," returning his tumbler to the table with an exasperated sigh. Antonio brought the water quickly, and the Captain resumed his glass, along with his smile, and the usual toast followed, "Here's luck," to which the other responded with its repetition.

At this moment Mercy came into the room, and Algie expected her to retire in disgust at sight of two men drinking together, with three other glasses standing half full upon the table. Instead, she manifested no surprise, but composedly took a seat by the fire. Before he was done with Blessington House he half wondered that she did not swear and drink also.

5

"Well, now, jest come straight to land.
I ain't much give to tackin' round a p'int.
How's it 'bout that pictur' you painted o' my
Mercy here ? "

Algie blushed and looked hopelessly at the
girl, who, surprised to find even the top of his
head sending a rosy gleam through his hair,
came to the rescue.

"Well, I—— " he had begun desperately.

"Oh, don't worry about it " exclaimed Mercy.
" I admired the little picture so much that I
told my father about it, and I did hope you
would be willing to part with it, and that he
might arrange for it."

" I told Mercy," said the Captain, interrupting her, " there ain't no use o' me a buyin' no
sech a scrap. When I wants somethin' I
wants it bad, and I don't want no trash.   Now
ef you could paint somethin' handsome !"—
indicating an unoccupied space upon the wall
where the pattern of the paper meandered
wearily through a large Arabesque design.

"Yes, yes, I understand. Something that
would fill a good space and be companionable," responded Algie.

Recovering himself, he wished that the old
man would leave him alone to talk to Mercy,
or that Mercy would leave him to her father.
He detested to be cornered into talking business before a woman. He looked appealingly
at her, and she promptly left the room.

" Bright girl," thought he, following her
with his eyes.

What man was there ever so susceptible as Algie! In love with the nursery maid at three years of age, he had never since been free from one thrall or another.

"Now, young man," began the Captain, "I 'lon't make no obligations I ain't got the money to meet; just name yer figur' and let it be reasonable. But let me say before ye begins that Solomon Blessin'ton ain't one as flings money aroun' broadcast. He knows the value o' every dollar; so name yer bottom price, an' let's hear."

"I can't see quite how it can be managed at all," replied Algie, who, although far from reluctant to take up the old man's offer, was anxious to cover his eagerness with the appearance of indifference; for already the romance of the situation had begun to work upon his fancy.

"How's that?" exclaimed the Captain, his face blank with surprise.

"Well, you see," answered Algie, who could sustain a part if necessary, "I already have some engagements; and then I haven't a studio which would do for a lady to pose in, and the weather is too unreliable to work out of doors; so, altogether, I don't quite see how——"

"Damn your studio!" interrupted the Captain excitedly. "Ain't Solomon Blessin'-ton's house good enough for a paint-shop?" —looking with pride around him.

"Oh, it would be quite out of the question,"

protested Algie, "I could not presume upon your hospitality."

"Now look a-here, young man," said the Captain gruffly, "the sooner you are satisfied to let well enough alone, the better for you. The little you'll eat here won't be nothin' to me, and you're welcome to it. You jes' make up yer min' and say what yer figur' is; I'm allus willin' to be far, but I don't want to be beholden to nobody, and I want yer to talk quick, and don't pester me, a-keepin' me a-waitin'!"

"Well," replied Algie reluctantly—he hated bargaining over his pictures, which were a part of his life, as if they were sticks or stones,—" well, I could not undertake it for less than three hundred dollars, and it would probably take me a month, and I'm afraid I should tire you out before that time."

The old man sat silent for a moment. He was reflecting. When he reflected, he yielded; this was invariable.

"Well, young man," said the Captain at length, with a sigh,—"I disremembers yer name, it's a oncommon one," he interpolated apologetically,—"long ez ye're here, and I don't 'spect to indulge no sich a extravagance agin soon, and I ain't got but one chile, and there ain't no tellin' how soon she'll want to be a-startin' a home o' her own, and gittin' away from mine, and seein' partic'lar ez she's sort o' sot her heart on it, I reckon ez how I'll agree."

All this peroration was intended to reconcile himself to what he thought was a personal extravagance.   And thus it came about
that Algernon Abercrombie found himself in
clover, and was paid for it, at the rate of three
hundred dollars a month, boarded and lodged,
and provided with a new heroine to entertain
his fickle fancy.   Who could blame him,
since the Captain had been eager to instate
him as the companion of his daughter, and to
pay him to study her day by day!   Alas!
the old Captain was making a venture without knowing the dangers of the game he was
playing.

No man was more sincere than Algernon.
He could not help being fickle, although, of
his own free will and accord, he had never
unloved one of his numerous flames.

Mercy, without being beautiful, had the
most winning and eloquent of faces, with
just enough pensiveness at times to inflame
the sympathy of his ardent temperament.
Having arranged to paint her, he felt priv-
ileged to study her, and there was a little
feeling of tender proprietorship in the smile
Algie gave her when she re-entered the
room.

"Well, Mercy, we's agreed!" announced
the Captain, with a similar look of ownership,
implying that the young artist belonged to
him for a month.

Mercy reassured Algie, who colored as he
looked at her, by saying: "I am very glad

indeed, very glad ; but do you know I have such a fancy for that pretty sketch of yester-day."

"So have I," replied Algernon, gaining confidence with her, "the tone is so good ; I fear I shall not get it again as well ! "

"What do artists mean by *tone ?* " inquired Mercy.

"I fear I cannot tell you easily," said he, studying the face before him. "If you look up the beach you will observe that the objects lose force, as well as color, until they fade into the haze of distance, or become too minute to be seen ; and that, however strong the contrast, they diminish equally. Now the preservation of the contrast of color with a just degree of diminution is meant by *sustaining the values.* A number of values so diminished are harmonious when they sustain each other without disagreement. In a grand piano a note is made of three strings, each of which is a value ; the three together form a tone, and several tones in satisfactory relation result in harmony. In painting, values which agree make harmony.

"Many harmonies sometimes exist in groups in a picture and combine into a greater coexistent harmony, which we call *tone.* Tone describes the average color of the whole picture. Transmute the idea ; take a rainbow, which is nature's picture on the sky. You· will have seven primary colors, which, although distinct, are of such equal value that they harmonize into a gray tone. Blue gray, yellow gray, red gray, green gray, and so forth. The tone of a rainbow is gray. A picture is low in tone, not by being dark, but by lacking accent, and being dull. It is high by reason of contrasts. High-toned pictures are more vivid, and have greater *chiaro oscuro*."

"And what is that?" exclaimed Mercy.

Algernon began to feel as if he had lent himself for a school-teacher, but it flattered his vanity all the same to have two earnest eyes fixed upon his face, and he was stimulated to proceed.

"That means light and shade," said he; "but not only the light and shade you see, but what you force in, to bring a stronger focus into the picture and prevent it from looking flat; because, when you paint from nature, you are obliged to take such a small part at a time of all you see that you often have to leave out the natural high light of the landscape, and therefore you force the picture by transferring to it something which you did not find in that place. When a picture is forced so much that it has only the fine things in the scene, and none of the commonplace ones, it loses its sincerity, and we say it is too *chic*, or 'goody-good.' Pictures exaggerated, either in light and shade or in tone or values, are more dramatic, but they are not simple and sincere and truthful."

Algie was very much in earnest as he uttered these last words, and paused, astonished to find that he had made so long a speech, while Mercy, looking at him kindly, said :

" I wish I could paint."

" You could not paint," said he, " without learning to draw ; color without form is deformity.   Still you are welcome to amuse yourself with my colors while I am here, and I will help you all I can ; but you would do much better to have a sketch-book and a blunt-pointed pencil, and reduce the tones and values to ' black and white.' "

Thus they laid plans for the future : he, enraptured with a new heroine, and full of the best intentions ; she interested in a new acquaintance, and ingenuous with the trust of a childlike innocence which knew absolutely nothing of the ways of the world.

CHAPTER VI.

ERCY'S eager attention flattered Algie, although he saw it was intellectual interest only, unleavened by desire for personal admiration. Such was the virgin coldness of her innocent smile, he could not believe it possible that passionate fervor could co-exist with such reserve. It is but justice to him, therefore, to say that, although he felt a great desire to win her esteem, he had no misgivings regarding the future, nor was there any unmanly vanity in his wish that she should think well of him.

Mercy sighed so heavily that Algie looked at her in surprise.

The needles had dropped from her fingers, and she stealthily brushed her eyes. She was experiencing that poignant self-rebuke one feels on awakening from a distraction to the memory of a great sorrow momentarily forgotten. She reproached herself with having enjoyed the talk of this pleasant stranger, who was nothing to her, while poor Jack at that moment might be suffering all manner of torments, even that of madness or death.

Algie thought her the most phenomenal

creature he had ever seen, and was at a loss
to account for such an hysterical transition,
until Mercy, perceiving his surprise, said to
him :

"Of course you do not know that we are
in despair about one of our vessels, and are
awfully distressed for the safety of the crew.
My foster-brother is the mate of the ship, and
his death would be insupportable."

"Oh, I dare say he'll turn up all right—
some day when you least expect him," said
Algie, feeling a cloud dim the sunshine of his
thoughts. Algernon was mercurial and became silent after a slight endeavor to cheer
Mercy, and fell to meditating upon the man
who had thus unexpectedly arisen. He found
himself a party to a romantic contract, bound
to devote himself to a lovely young woman,
whose duties to himself as hostess and model
were quite as imperative and stringent. He
did not feel pleased at the prospect of a rival
with eighteen years the start of him, since
eighteen years against one day is a race sadly
at odds. It was a strong proof of his kindness of heart that he devoted his ingenuity to
devising possible and plausible coincidences
which might have conspired to promote Jack's
rescue and salvation, all vividly portrayed with
an eloquent tongue and a marvellous voice. I
dwell upon Algie's voice, because it was his
great gift and his great responsibility as well.

He could not have chosen a more certain
manner of winning the girl's heart. She

really needed a youthful friend. Jack was
the only friend she had ever had, except
Mother Margery. Algernon, judging her
as a stranger, thought he had discovered a
secret; but he was wrong in supposing the
rough mate of the "Marianetta" to be her
lover, declared or undeclared. Such a
thought had not entered her mind. Jack had
not dared lift his hopes so high. She was
and had ever been an idol to him, which he
never expected to woo from the safe-keeping
of its present shrine. Worship forbids equal-
ity, and this idolatry in a rude way was worship, the worship of a great physical power
for an exalting moral one ; and Mercy knew
she must miss that devotion which had never
failed in its constancy and faith.

Had she known more of men, she would
have discovered speedily that Algie was
much too impatient of trifles to render her
such daily and hourly homage. He con-
densed mighty emotions into a few days of exaggerated passion, which ended in nothing
save remorse or disgust. No woman had
hitherto been found with sufficient far-sighted
courage to wait with faith for the Phœnix to
arise from the ashes, believing that it would
arise.

Algernon was capable of living a nobler
life than he had lived ; but he needed the
stimulant of hourly contact with a more consistent nature—or, at all events, one strong
where he was weak. Mercy's truth and

purity appealed divinely to his imagination. She could not conceive of inconstancy since she had never known it, and during his stay at Cassandra she showed such faith in the sincerity of every word he uttered as almost to drive him wild, since he could not quite decide whether it resulted from indifference or confidence, forbearance or contempt. The pendulum of his heart beat to and fro, with ever a settling to the mean distance.

Algie's fickleness had hitherto been a constant cause of anxiety to his friends, although it was the result of fastidiousness and impatience, rather than shallowness and want of force, as they had imagined. Many a man, of great and varied powers, fails through want of a single quality which another person, closely allied to him, might unconsciously supply. His extravagances were a subject of censure as well, and it is to be feared that New Year's Day too often found the generous vagabond with a balance-sheet weighing heavily the wrong way.

Still he was accounted a good fellow, whom every one loved with too genuine a feeling to be quite willing to speak ill of; and even that may be worth something in the long run; since he that is not against us is for us, although it is to be regretted that those who had been the objects of his generosity had not found occasion to make good words available.

The Captain, meanwhile, had been agi-

tated to a fresh realization of his responsibility as a father, by Aunt Polly, who, not
having come under the seduction of Algie's
charming manner, had vehemently assailed
the judiciousness of the Captain's hospitable
intentions ; finally asserting, with angry ve-
hemence, that he had gone out of his way,
with childish giddiness, to drag a stranger
into the house, whose threadbare coat was
proof sufficient that he was a tramp.

"All the more need of a chance to earn
his bread," the Captain protested.

"He might be the most corrupt person in
the world ! " Aunt Polly insisted. "Here
are Mercy and I, exposed to the contamina-
tions of a wandering vagabond, who might
have no moral character. Indeed, Solomon,
it is wickedness ; I can call it by no other
name ! "

"Now look-a-here, Polly, do ye s'pose I
don't know men, and can't tell a gentleman
when I lay my eyes on him ? " exclaimed the
Captain, exasperated ; and, turning impatiently away, he started with surprise at seeing
three pair of eyes in a row blinking through
the mess-room door, slightly ajar. Now the
Captain knew very well that, in the secret
places of their hearts, the three old shipmates
detested Aunt Polly ; and there was a child-
like satisfaction to the skipper in the knowledge that even if Aunt Polly got the better
of him, somebody was taking his part, and he

felt suddenly robust with moral support and returned to the charge.

Aunt Polly, changing her tactics, granted that the artist might be a gentleman, but she assured the Captain that, if he were, Mercy would certainly fall in love with him. The Captain was too obtuse to see anything monstrous in that idea, and the three sailors listened with increased interest.

But the Captain's curiosity being equal to Aunt Polly's imagination, he determined to settle the matter at once, and proceeded to the dining-room, which in winter was used as a common sitting-room as well. Finding Mercy and Algie in what seemed a suspiciously confidential attitude, that is, Mercy reclining in her chair, and Algernon leaning eagerly forward, still holding his hat in his hand, he might have felt there was some truth in Aunt Polly's prognostication, had not the sadness in Mercy's face contradicted it, and the extreme deference of Algie's manner reassured him.

"Um, well, aw— !" began the Captain with such evident embarrassment that even Mercy looked up with surprise, "Mr. Abercorn, I wuz a-thinkin' that you ain't got no stuff here to work on, and I've got some sort o' business what'll take me to town, to Richmond more'n like, and it struck me of a sudden p'raps you'd like ter go 'long and fetch 'em."

The Captain smiled self-approvingly, for he had conceived the plan of making it his business

to find out all there was to know about the
unconscious Algernon, although that person
would have been quite equal to giving a pretty
bad account of himself. As events proved,
however, the victim of this plot gained considerably by it ; for, as I have said, Algie's
friends were sufficiently bound to him to
bestow a good word when they had nothing
more convertible.

" But, really," began Algie, reddening, " I
am in such a plight I could not present myself
with you in Richmond."

The Captain's brow clouded, but he was a
man of such habitual kindness that it quickly
cleared. " Well, I ain't proud," he replied,
looking at the young man with self-evident
compassion.

Algie smiled to himself. " An Oyster Cove
skipper ashamed to be seen in company
with Mr. Algernon Abercombie. What next !"
His mother would have said it " served him
just right for mixing himself up with such
vulgar people ! " But when he looked at his
old painting-coat, as ragged as it was comfortable, he began to feel a little of the wonder
of a stranger's eyes.

" My dear Mr. Blessington ! " he cried
deprecatingly, " I am so ashamed to have put
in such an appearance, but my clothes are at
a tavern near the station, and I fear, if I should
delay to make a change, you would miss the
train, and that would interfere with your
plans. Really you must allow me to return

to my lodgings and make myself presentable. I did not expect to meet a lady when I left this morning."

" Ah, indeed," exclaimed the Captain, in some confusion, berating Aunt Polly in his secret mind, but casting about wildly for something to say. Pulling out his big watch by way of diversion, he regarded it studiously. " No, it ain't late. I'll have her got ready, and we'll go over thar in no time at all, and ye ken jes' fetch yer tackle here and make yourself at home, like, don't ye know ? "

" Certainly," replied Algernon, with well-feigned alacrity, although he would have much preferred spending the morning with Mercy to rushing off to Richmond with this blustering old mariner. But it was a consolation to know that it would soon be done and over with, so he made the most of the short interval before the Captain summoned him. He could not resist turning back at the last moment to give her a parting glance. Hospitality alone prompted Mercy to say, " I hope you will be back early to-morrow, Mr. Abercrombie."

Aunt Polly, prim and severe, was just entering the doorway, and, overhearing her remark, looked at the Captain with the most " I-told-you-so " expression, and afterward gazed stonily at the young man as if he were a thief.

Algernon, at all times over-sensitive, colored until he was crimson, and his hair and moustache stood out in relief like new bronze. Mercy's instinct to protect was as ready as her compassion, and, knowing the meaning of Aunt Polly's lofty mien, came forward promptly.

"Aunt Polly," said she, "you have not met my pleasant acquaintance of yesterday; this is Mr. Abercrombie, who has been so very good as to promise to paint my portrait."

Aunt Polly bowed grimly, and Algie, recovering himself, gave Mercy a look of unutterable gratitude.

"This here young man an' me's a goin' to the city to fetch home some things; and, Mercy, you jes' tell Splugen to put her in the gig while I go up an' shave, and holler for Tony to fetch the hot water. Long ez ye ain't got yer clean close here, Mr. *What's-yer-name*, jes' set down and make yerself comfortable by the fire till I get dressed."

Algie, having mistaken the Captain's nod, which had been intended for Mercy, and perceiving that he was expected to return to the fireside, followed Aunt Polly.

When Mercy came back, she found him endeavoring to make himself agreeable, and failing utterly.

Aunt Polly sat, grimly assertive of her own virtue and immaculateness.

Her hair was rolled smoothly over round combs upon each side of her pale forehead. Her collar was wide and white and very stiff, and would have choked any other person, but

6

her face was bloodless. Her eyes were of a light, uninspired blue ; and her white hands were folded upon her lap.

" By Jove ! " Algie was thinking, " this is more than I bargained for ! It is a mistake to give the sweet first, and the bitter afterwards." He suspected, shrewdly enough, that his old coat was his evil genius ; so he began making apologies.

" I was just saying to Mr. Blessington, madame, that I was ashamed to have put in such an appearance ; but I came out this morning intending to work very hard ; and when that happens, I dare not trust myself in decent clothes, or I should live at my tailor's."

Aunt Polly relented a little, and cast upon him a half-inquiring glance.

" I am ever and always shocking my mother. She declares I ought to belong to a junk-shop," he added, seeing she did not speak.

" You have found your destination here," said Mercy laughing, " for I have been thinking you might use father's lumber-room for a studio. It's the most awful place at present. Would you like to see it ? Won't you come too, Aunt Polly ? " she added, rising and leading the way.

Aunt Polly was too much amazed at Mercy's forwardness to reply, and Algie, frantic to escape, followed precipitately. She crossed the hall, and, opening the opposite door, they entered a long room. It held, in outlandish mixture, the probable gleanings of a seafaring life heaped in the corners, about the floor, or rudely piled against the walls.

"I have so often wished I could arrange these," said Mercy, after allowing Algie time to look around.

"By Jove!" he exclaimed, "what fine properties for a studio! If you say so, and your father is willing, we will do these things up magnificently before we begin the picture at all."

"I will see if I can persuade him, but you must leave it entirely to me. These queer things have all been brought to him by sailors he has befriended, for my father has a very kind heart."

"In the mouth of many witnesses," quoted Algernon, who was fond of making quotations and never made them accurately.

"Father never would quite consent to let me arrange them, but, if you help me, he may."

"I will show him my studio," said Algernon with pardonable pride, at the same time casting his eyes, with the practised knowledge of an artist, over the extraordinary collection of things, both hideous and beautiful, which lay in dusty confusion about him.

His face shone with pleasure, as if he would have enjoyed going to work then and there, but at that very moment the Captain was heard descending the stairs, talking to himself; and Algie, being alone with Mercy, impulsively offered his hand to bid her good-bye.

" You will certainly see me again," said he, turning toward Aunt Polly, who was standing in the hall, " for you know I am leaving the best part of me behind."

Aunt Polly was scandalized and looked reproachfully at the young man, who, in truth, did not mean his heart, but his paint-box.

CHAPTER VII.

LGERNON experienced some difficulty in accommodating himself to
the small space which remained in
the gig, the Captain having further
increased the amplitude of his stout figure by
arraying himself in an enormous Irish driv-
ing-coat with capes, which was a part of the
collection. But, being determined to make
the most of his situation, Algie clung tenaciously to the back of the gig, half-embracing
the Captain.

The old skipper had conceived a wonderful
liking for the younger man, and when he
came forth from his lodging dressed in the
perfection of fashion, he sighed to think he
could not take him bodily and present him to
Aunt Polly.

It was late when they reached Richmond,
and the train slowed up for the long bridge.
The red glow from the iron-works gleamed
across the river, and the lights of the city
sparkled like fire-flies in the hollows of its
hills.

"I hope you won't mind my leaving you
at my studio for a little while," said Algie
to the Captain, "and after that we'll have a
snug little dinner together. Here we are,"

he added, a few minutes later, as the carriage drew up at the curbstone.

When he had opened the door of his studio with a key from his pocket, he touched a button, and the room became instantly ablaze with electric light. The Captain was paralyzed with wonder. To his eyes, confused by the sudden change from the darkness, it was like a scene from the "Arabian Nights."

Algie loved luxury, and had been rash enough, upon his coming of age, to cut a slice from his inheritance and deliberately invest it in what his friends called "trash." He could not dispute their wisdom, but had maintained that ugliness shortened life and limited intelligence ; and ugly things, as household gods, he could not have.

The Captain, by instinct, had good taste, and the young artist felt great satisfaction in watching him as he walked around, handling the heathenish bric-a-brac, exclaiming at intervals, "Well, I never !"

"You'll have time for a good rest," said Algie, assisting him to remove his coat, "and what would you say to a brandy *smash ?*"

"I'm agreeable !" said the Captain, without coquetry, settling himself in a very large arm-chair and passing his hands through his white hair, until it stood on end.

Algie rang for his servant, and placed the Captain under his care before leaving.

Chance, or Mr. Algernon Abercrombie, developed the Captain's plot.

"Go seek a man's valet, if you would know the man."

The old skipper sipped his grog, as he stared into the newly-lighted fire, smiling to himself the while, and admiring his own shrewdness. But Algernon Abercrombie would not have been himself if he could not put Aunt Polly and the old painting-coat together, and have worked out the combination.

"Does all these here things belong to this here young man?" inquired the Captain of Jarvis.

"Yes, sir; an' lots more beside, an' more's always a-comin'!"

"How's that?" said the Captain, wondering.

"He's such a favor*ite* with the ladies, sir. There ain't hardly a day passing but brings something for a present. He's a gentleman, sir, of the choicest. There ain't no more of a gentleman in this here town of Richmond; that's the reverend truth for sure."

"Don't he have no men folks for frien's?" inquired the Captain uneasily, feeling some misgivings about the fulfilment of Aunt Polly's prophecy.

"Oh, yes, sir! Indeed he do," answered Jarvis, brushing a few motes of dust off the mantelpiece with his forefinger. "He's got more of them poor artists runnin' after him than it pays him to have. I was a-sayin' yestiddy to Mr. Jinks, what waits below, that

Mr. Abercrombie was *too* good-natured—kind-
hearted, so to speak—for his own accumula-
tion.   He's one o' them sort as is too much of
a gentleman to take proper keer of theirselves.
He's always gittin' imposed upon !   Why, sir,
you kin believe me if you choose, but if *I*
didn't take keer of him he wouldn't have
nothin' ! "

'The Captain eyed his empty glass and
sighed.   " You ain't got no good ole Jamaiky,
is ye ? " he said at length.

" I'm afeared I ain't," said Jarvis, " but
here's various sorts," he added, rather pompously, pulling aside the curtain of mandarin
yellow brocade which hung across the cupboard door.

" How's it that yer young man don't take
one o' them gals en anchor by her ?   I
reckon if he did, t'others might let him have a
chance ter war out them slippers."

" Well, sir," answered Jarvis, dropping his
voice mysteriously, " it do seem sometimes ez
ef it wa'n't nothin' but contrariness ; but I
'lows he's kinder choice.   I reckon he ain't
found one yet as'll please him satisfactory.
Then, agin, I 'lows he's sp'ilt, they all makes
such a fuss over him, continual."

Meanwhile Algernon had found his way to
his mother's dressing-room, where, robed in a
black satin *peignoir*, with a towel across her
shoulders, she sat, submitting to having her
hair dressed for a dinner-party.

" I told you so, Algernon," she was saying.

"I knew there was a girl at the bottom of it."

"What I came to say," replied her son, ignoring her remark, "is, that the Captain has agreed to give me three hundred dollars for painting the picture of his daughter, and it will save me a lot of expense for a month, besides putting money in my pocket. Moreover, I shall have a good rest and keep early hours and be with the kindest people in the world. A new state of things, you must confess, for me."

"What sort of people are they?" inquired his mother anxiously.

"As common as they make 'em! That is, all except the daughter, who is the purest-looking girl I ever saw. The old skipper owns a number of vessels and a fleet of oyster smacks; and there is an old maiden aunt who is a living terror, a small maid who is never to be found, three old sailors, a hideous brown dog, and a green parrot. All live in a big brick house in the sand-hills, where it is as lonely as the North Pole and just about as primitive. But the Captain's a jolly old torpedo, with a voice like a roaring tempest and a smooth red face like a big baby's. I know you'd like him. Do let me bring him around in the morning!"

"My child!" exclaimed Mrs. Abercrombie in dismay. "I couldn't receive the man before breakfast. Couldn't he come up another time? I am so sorry to refuse you."

"Well, go with me to the studio this evening, and let me show you off before dinner, you would give me no end of a character!"

"What time is it now?" inquired Mrs. Abercrombie, hesitating.

"Only a quarter-past seven."

"But I am to dine at half-past eight."

He finally overcame her reluctance, and persuaded her to make the time for him, and they presently set out together.

"Now, my dear boy," she said, when they were in the coupe, "promise me not to fall in love with this Captain's daughter. If you only knew the anxiety so many love-affairs cost me! Positively, it keeps me awake at night."

"Now look here, mother, if you talk like that, I'll believe you're jealous. Mothers are such selfish creatures!" answered Algie, laughing. "But here we are, and do be nice to him,—I want to make an impression."

"An impression on whom, the mariner or the mermaid?" said she, taking his hand to get out of the carriage. Algie did not reply, but busied himself with holding the train of her gown as she crossed the sidewalk and ascended the stairs.

When they reached the studio the lights were still lowered, and the Captain asleep. Jarvis was nowhere to be seen.

Algie and Mrs. Abercrombie had the advantage of the situation.

When the old skipper discovered them he started to his feet with a bound, astonished to find himself in the presence of a beautiful woman. He rubbed his eyes, and shook himself to see if he were dreaming, pulling down his waistcoat and smoothing his hair to make himself presentable.

"Captain Blessington," said Mrs. Abercrombie, taking a step forward, and offering her hand to the Captain, who received it like an oyster, and let it slip out of his grasp, "my son tells me that he is going to you for a month, and I came down for a moment to see you, and beg you to take good care of him."

"There ain't nothin' to hurt him, ma'am," answered the Captain artlessly ; " he ain't sickly, I hope ? " taking his spectacles out of a tin box and putting them on to look at Algie.

" He tells me you have a fine large house. I thought there was nothing but barren sand at Cassandra Bay."

" It's come by boat, ma'am. I like things solid an' comfortable, and don't go in fur show without no foundation. Reg'lar ole Virginny ; I ain't got nothin' fine, ma'am—'lessen 'tis my Mercy. I do count her 'bout ez fine a young un ez steps 'long our parts. Got lots o' solid nat'ral sense. Not ez I goes in fur praisin' my own flesh an' blood."

Mrs. Abercrombie, worldly though she might be, looked in appreciative surprise upon the Captain as he swelled with pleasure and pride at thought of Mercy, and she and her son exchanged glances.

" I wish it were possible for me to stay and
see more of you ; but I am late as it is, and I
dared allow myself but two minutes to meet
you." She looked at her watch, suddenly recollecting the dinner-party. " I am obliged to
say good-bye ; but some day, when you're in
town, you will let me have the pleasure of
seeing you again, I know."

She shook hands with the Captain, who was
considering her appearance with a good deal
of wonder.

Her hair, without a trace of silver ; her
beautiful white throat, relieved by lace from
too severe contrast with the black dress ; the
elegance and grace of her figure, as round
and erect as in youth ; and the almost lover-
like pride with which her son regarded her,
—were altogether different from the Captain's
preconceived ideas of a woman of fifty.

For once in his life he cursed his luck that
he had not Aunt Polly by the ear to say to
her, " I told you so !" However, it would
bear repeating.

Algie accompanied his mother to her carriage and then returned to escort his guest to
dinner.

The next morning, a few minutes before
train time, both men were at the station ready
to return to Cassandra Bay.

It was with a sigh of heartfelt relief that
the younger man turned his back upon
the city, with its life of debt and dissipation,
and abandoned himself to the enjoyment

of a month's immunity from care and temptation.

He was free-hearted and lavish, and loved to be thought well of by others, and he knew for a truth that his injudicious extravagances had been for the benefit of others rather than himself; but his heart sickened none the less at the harvest which awaited him, and it was with satisfaction that he left his own home, with its singular complication of pride, affection, affectation, and extravagance, and looked happily forward to a new field, where none but harmless paths enticed his steps under the reposeful and ennobling influence of Mercy's presence; for if Mercy had seemed brusque and self-asserting to him at first, she had lingered in his memory with the refreshment of an ocean breeze arousing an unknown energy. Life at Blessington House had a meaning, and each individual a purpose; and Algie, whose years hitherto had been spent in getting rid of time, began to experience a new and different interest in casting his lot with theirs, or, more accurately, with one who, young as she was, seemed to have accepted, as her mission in life, the effort to make better, by the stimulus of her personal sympathy, all who came about her. He dimly realized that all men approach their fellows with a purpose,—the purpose to be admired, the purpose to be loved, the purpose to rule. Having an affectionate nature, he could not rest satisfied until he made the thing which was near him love him ; and the interest which he had devoted to that effort even he had mistaken for love. He now proposed to spend a month in the proximity of a woman too noble for coquetry, and too generous in her estimate of others not to give him more credit for virtue than he deserved.

In their mutual relation, she was interested, and he was eager.

Unquestionably it gave her pleasure to see the easel and paint-box in the corner, where they stood in surety of his return.

The sun was shining, but the ragged clouds scudding across the sea gave feeble assurance of spring in face of the rigors of winter which remained, when the tramp of the old horse was heard upon the shells, and the Captain's voice shouting for Splugen.

The whole house revived as from a slumber. Sailor wagged his tail against the Captain's shins, and howled with joy ; the green parrot screamed, and moved excitedly from one leg to the other, as if on hot iron ; Antonio and Bill Junk, on the watch for something to turn up, were staring out of the window with their noses flattened against the pane. Algie, perceiving that Mercy and Aunt Polly were above, lifted his hat, and hurried indoors out of the wind.

CHAPTER VIII.

LGIE looked so well-dressed when he entered the sitting-room that Aunt Polly was struck mute with surprise, and put out her hand, almost unwittingly, to greet him.

" I hope you will forgive my wearing my overcoat to the fire, but I am so cold ! " said he, shaking hands in turn with each of the ladies. After a few moments he removed the coat and threw it carelessly over the back of a chair, so that its satin lining gleamed in the light, while he stood shivering and warming his hands over the grate. He was exceptionally well dressed, and his cut-away fitted him to a nicety. His hair, fresh from the barber, was fine, smooth, gleaming, and faintly perfumed ; as if lately washed in eau de cologne, and of a beautiful golden red,— much too lovely for a man ! His full moustache, worn rather long, and his firm, almost obstinate chin, were marked features of a face and head massively put together, and well set upon the shoulders.

" It was so nice of you to come back to do the picture," said Mercy, with a kindliness which showed her quite mistress of the situation, and also made Algie conscious that he had left no impression upon her.

His vanity was piqued to its supremest effort ; and he felt his interest increase with the sense of resistance.

" Work in any other form, Miss Blessington, was never a temptation to me," said he gallantly, as he took up his coat to lay it aside.

" Don't trouble about the coat, Mr. Abercrombie," said Aunt Polly, now all effusion, " Antonio will take it to your room, and the Captain will send Splugen for your luggage."

" You are much kinder to me than I deserve——"

" There ain't no use talkin' 'bout it," exclaimed the Captain, jerking the door open and blustering in ; " I'll be sent to a better place—" (this was the occasional compromise under Mercy's efforts to reform his desire to go to a worse) "—ef I ain't a-gittin' a spell o' rheumatiz this very minute. Mercy, whar's that gal ? Come here and pull off my shoes. Where's them slippers ? "

Mercy brought the slippers and, much to Algie's astonishment, sat down on the floor at her father's feet.

Aunt Polly detested such familiarity and left the room. Then the Captain spread himself, like a vast human wonder, in his big chair before the fire, and there seemed nothing left for Algie to do but to sit down in another.

With the unaffectedness of a child Mercy unlaced her father's big shoes, exchanging them for his slippers, and, perhaps out of deference to Algie, made an effort to arise.

"Rub them ankle-bones!" cried the Captain sententiously, closing his eyes and turning his head away from the light. Mercy removed the slippers again and proceeded to rub her father's feet, whilst Algie amused himself with alternately looking into the fire and studying the Captain, until at length his eyes rested upon Mercy, who must have forgotten him. It goaded his pride that she should sit cuddling a sleepy old man, even though he were her father, whilst he, the invincible Algernon Abercrombie, was present.

After a while it struck him that she was very patient with the old skipper in this singular demand; though it exasperated him to see her scorching her face painfully.

He did not remember that she had told him she gained her influence with her father in big things by sacrificing herself to him in little things. She sat down near him, but, after a very few moments, seemed to be oblivious to all about her. He wondered if this habitual absent-mindedness was not due to an effort her mind made to escape from irksome and uncongenial surroundings.

Her face in the firelight had such a look of sweet endurance as to confirm the thought, although her whole manner, when speaking, tended to draw his attention to the best in the people and things about her, and the very effort to hide her own individuality threw a

7

veil of mystery about it which perplexed him.

She did not strike him as "goody-good," but as having that sort of forbearance which nothing human could shock, and which gave to her character the quality of moral toughness.

"Shan't I ring for Antonio?" inquired Mercy. "Wouldn't you like to go to your room and rest for a few moments? I fear you will find it stupid here; for father always sleeps an hour at least when he has been out in the cold."

"Oh!" replied Algie, delighted at the prospect, "I had much rather spend that hour with you, even in grim silence."

"I can amuse myself with my knitting," said Mercy.

"Do you knit every day?" inquired Algie. "Such stupid work!" he added, with a man's contempt for monotony.

"No, indeed!" said she, "I am so fond of reading, that I read or study every day; but when I am worried or uneasy—and we, who have friends at sea, must be so at times—I knit, because the stupid repetition seems to rest my brain."

"Your father brought you no news; but 'no news is good news,'" said he kindly.

"If you comfort me with proverbs, I must answer that 'hope deferred maketh the heart sick.'"

"What use can you make of so much

knitted work ? " said Algie, anxious to change the subject.

"Oh, I knit these long comforters, and the men take them to sea. I think they have a little sentiment about my work, although perhaps that is vanity. When it happens that they never come back again, I am glad that I gave them a piece of my own work before they went."

"You must think about such lots of things when you are knitting, only I can't conceive what you can have to think about, your life is so lonely."

"I am not necessarily lonely because I am isolated," said Mercy, looking up surprised, and encountering a commiserating sympathy in his eyes which made her drop her own ; but she immediately aroused herself to resist his influence, and added, "so long as I know that some one depends upon me, I can never feel quite useless or alone. The necessities of others make me a necessity to my position. I have no time to be idle, therefore no time to be lonely."

Algie withheld a hasty compliment, which seemed too trivial to offer to one so in earnest.

If Algie thought her life lonely, he might have suspected that words of appreciation were rarer still than friends.

But Mercy's character seemed so well balanced and complete, that, out of the very reverence he felt for her, he ignored the natural craving of her human necessities. Thus it seems at times, that those who struggle after a high ideal must be satisfied to meet with no other approval than that of their own consciences.

" Is there a fire in the other room ? " he asked abruptly, indicating the one containing her father's collection.

" No," said Mercy, " would you like one ? " " Oh, no, I only thought that if there were, we might look over the things together ; but I like it immensely here with you, and, if you don't mind, while you knit, I will sketch you in my book. I will be so silent that you could think the sky full of thoughts. So saying, Algie took a book from his pocket, and, sharpening his pencil bluntly, put in a very broad line sketch.

" Do you always carry a book ? "

" Yes, it is such fine practice, and then, too, it is pleasant to be able to illustrate accounts of my expeditions when I get home, especially to mother. For example, if I told her that your father was asleep in his chair, and you were sitting beside him knitting yarn comforters, and making me feel very happy and at home near you, my words would not make half the impression which this little sketch would."

" Do you know," said Mercy naively, " that I have always so longed to know an artist ? I am so fond of pictures, and there seems such a mystery in their creation, that it is quite an ideal thing for me to have you thus sitting be-side the fire and sketching even me, without

jarring in the least upon my humdrum life ;
except that I have dropped this stitch through
thinking of your work instead of mine,"

" I wish you would drop it all through such
a fault ! " exclaimed Algie impulsively.

Mercy looked at him with a smile and
said : " I might, if you held the key of the
North Pole, and could promise there should
be no more cold noses or aching ears. But
since you cannot, I shall have to pick it up
again."

If she had simpered, Algie would have been
bored, but the fact that his flattery was ridic-
ulous to her nettled him.

" When we get father's room all to rights,
you can always come here and paint whenever you want to sketch at Cassandra. We'd
all like it, you know. It'll be much better
than tumbling around in the wind on the top
of a sand-hill. Moreover, I'm going to watch
you paint, and then I shall try too."

It touches a man at his weakest to be
imitated by any one, but when his mimic is a
young and pretty girl it turns his brain. Algie
cast upon Mercy, quite thoughtlessly, another
of his tender glances.

" You think you can persuade your father
to let us, don't you ? " A slight softening of
the voice made that " us " sound very pleasant
in Mercy's ear. The exchange of you and me,
for we and us, was an appreciable pleasure to
Algie, which Mercy perceived without understanding ; though she blushed slightly, and

his heart, which had been warming steadily, melted as it had done so often before.

Ere the drowsy old Captain awoke, Algie, without thought of harm, but prompted by the desire to be fully in sympathy with all who came near him, had exerted himself to impress a nature which was not susceptible, but which, having conceived, never lost even the memory of an affection ; whilst he, luxuriating in the love he habitually inspired, took no thought of the future, and could not believe that he must hoard his friends as well as his money against a day of want. It was quite sufficient for him to be happy. At that moment he desired nothing more for happiness than to have Mercy beside him, developing new charms for himself alone.

Something of this happiness was visible in the little sketch growing under his pencil, for even that was lovingly done. He had put into it the grace of Mercy's bending head, and her own sweet look of protective benignity, as if her heart were a sanctuary where the weary found help to rest them, and the disappointed, the wicked, or the wavering might find consolation or encouragement to do better.

At times a pang of remorse tightened the chords of her heart, for, whilst she hoped for the best for poor Jack, there arose between her and her memories of him, mingling with her sorrow, a faint sweet sense of satisfaction in the present, which the loyalty of her heart resented.

Had Mercy known more of the world and understood that sincerity was no proof of constancy; that the meteor, while it lasts, is just as real as the star,—she would have been on the defensive ; but, by defending herself, she would have lost the confiding innocence which was her charm in Algie's eyes.

He continued silent and absorbed, finishing his sketch, with Mercy knitting quietly near him, till the Captain awoke with a start which brought him to his feet.

"Father," said Mercy, "we've been laying a trap for you ! "

"Well," said he, with a growl, "is that anything new ? "

"Yes, very new indeed ; we want to get up a studio."

"What the devil is that for ? " he exclaimed in astonishment.

"Because I want to learn to paint, and while Mr. Abercrombie is here it would be so awfully nice if you would let us have your room for him to paint my picture in. We would put all of your things in order and make it so comfortable. *Now*, it's a regular old caravansary."

"Them things pleases me jest so," said the Captain demurely, feeling rather insulted.

"But they'd do you much more good if they were dusted and hung up ; and when your old friends came to visit you, they would see that you set some store by their presents.

Indeed, it would be a great thing for you if you only knew it ! "

" Lord, jest hear her talk ! " cried the skipper, looking helplessly from one to the other.

" Yes," said Algie sympathetically.

" Did you ever hear a gal talk like that ? " her father asked, looking for protection—even beguiled into imploring it—from Algie.

" Never," said the young man gravely.

" No, nor nobody else," said the Captain, sitting down. " A stoody fur me ! when it takes purty nigh all the strength an' enterprise I got to keep alongside o' her ! Confound it, I couldn't do nothin' with it ef I had it."

" It would be a good place to eat apples," suggested Mercy.

The Captain wiped his spectacles, after taking them down from the top of his head, put them on again, and looked at her in surprise.

" I can eat apples, or anything else convenient, right whar I be, always providin' I got an apple and an appetite."

" I don't mean to limit you ; I only mean that while Mr. Abercrombie paints, you can eat apples or smoke, or otherwise entertain me, to induce a smiling expression."

" Why can't we do jest the same right here ? "

" Because there are so many interruptions all the time, and not space enough. Mr. Abercombie would be certain to tread upon Aunt Polly's toes."

" I wish to the Lord he would ! " exclaimed

the Captain devoutly. After a moment's silence he added, " I'll be blowed, if I won't thank the Lord Almighty when I kin git a place to myself ; if it ain't mor'n six feet long ; whar, when I do settle down, there won't be nobody to pester me ! Why, Mr. What's-yer-name. there ain't been a day sence this here Mercy's been born, that she ain't imposed on me for somethin'. Little or big, it's etarnal somethin'. When she was a baby, she begun it with cryin' for a coral stick off'n my watch-chain what I was a-carryin' for luck, an' she would have it, an' I give in ! She got it, 'cause I was afeared she would die if she didn't git it ; and it's jest got to be all my life's worth to cross her. Ef she's sot her heart on a thing she can't rest, nor let no body rest, 'tell she's got it. Now this here pictur' o' yourn is a fair sample o' her doin's. She's jest a turnin' of me bodily out'n the house, and me gittin old too."

" It does look like it," said Algie solemnly.

Tears sprang into Mercy's eyes, and her mouth quivered like a child's.

The Captain looked from one to the other scowling. This remark of Algie's showed very clever insight into the character of the skipper ; for as soon as he found any one willing to take part against Mercy, he turned bodily over to her side whether the argument was for or against himself.

" Humph ! " said the skipper ; " what did you say, young man ? "

"I said it did look a little that way," replied Algie, deprecatingly.

"Well, I don't exactly know, young man, whether it do or not. Speak up, Mercy, ain't you got no tongue? Do you mean to sit thar, and hear this here young man accusin' you o' turnin' your ole daddy out o' doors? What's you got to say for yerse'f?"

"You know I don't," replied Mercy, almost with a sob, and furtively drying her tears. "I want to turn you in; for you never go in there now, except to take some old sailor to see a tortoise-shell, or a fish-net; and, if we could make it pleasant, you could get out of the way when things are not quite right here."

"Then where the devil would you go?"

"Of course I'd go there with you. It's big enough for two of us, gracious knows!"

"Now why couldn't you say that at first," exclaimed the Captain, smiling suddenly. "You're a sharp young one, jest fixin' a way to git rid o' Polly. I know'd it! Take me for findin' out what a gal's up to!"

He chuckled delightedly to himself, and turned half round to the others, bubbling over with satisfaction. "Why can't you speak confidential-like to your ole daddy, an' not be a-makin' a strange young man think you're tryin' to hurry him off?"

"You dear old darling, you will, won't you?" cried Mercy, jumping up and throwing her arms around his neck, and giving him two sounding kisses, at which Algie almost fainted.

"Now did you ever see the likes o' that?" inquired the Captain with pride, turning a beaming countenance upon Algie, who admitted that he had never been obliged to witness anything of that sort before. The old fellow enjoyed being the hero of domestic episodes, though he assumed a look of endurance which was almost tragic.

"Young man," said he severely, "take my advice, and don't never let yourse'f begin to be bossed by a woman, for jest 'as the twig is bent the tree inclines.'"

"Yes," said Algie demurely, "but I can't say I'd mind being bent that way."

"Say you're going to let us," insisted Mercy.

"Did I ever have a say about nothin',— ever once, sence you was born?"

"Well, granted. Will you wait to begin next time?"

"Lord-a-massy, I never seed sich a gal! Talk about wills; there ain't no man livin' what can hold a candle 'longside o' some women. They're that persistent they're *tejus!*"

"But you say yes, and it'll be over with."

"It's worse than havin' a tooth pulled, I declar! I ain't had no time to consider. But it's a clean waste of breath to argue a p'int with a woman. They ain't got no judgment. What the Lord ever made a man with

two women for, I don't know. Here's my
Mercy, insistin' all the week, and Polly with
her prayer-book, exortin' all of a Sunday. I
ain't even got no prospect o' peace. For Mercy's a-persecutin' me for my worldly posses-
sions from Monday mornin' 'tell Sadday night,
and Polly is a-tellin' of me all day Sunday
that I ain't got no treasure laid up nowhar.
I'll be damned if they leaves me even a expectation of a chance ! "

" It *is* pretty rough," replied Algie.

" I should think it were ; and, young man,
jest you take a ole man's advice and let 'em
alone.   Let 'em alone ! "

" That's easier said than done," said the
young man.

" You're right about that.   For I tell you,
if you give 'em a inch, they're sure to take a
ell, and it's a long ways the best sailin' not
to give 'em no inch.   Tack about, but don't
let 'em land you nowhars ! "

" Well, if that is what you really think, and
you don't care anything about me, I can let
you alone," said Mercy.

" Who said I wa'nt goin' to let you have no
inch ?   I was advisin' this here young gentleman for his own good.   Ain't I dun let you
take my room, and all my things for a stoody ?
Ain't I goin' to have you a pretty pictur'
painted ?   Who says I ain't willin' to give you
the las' cent I got, ef I had to go a thousan'
miles to fetch it.   And, positively, I ain't allowed so much as the privilege o' complainin' ! "

"Oh, he should, that he should!" cried Mercy, cuddling him, "but all the same, we may have the room?"

"Ain't I said Yes? How many times is I got to repeat it? You know you ain't a-goin' to leave off 'tell you get yer way, and what's the use o' so much pesterin'?"

"Yes, but I don't want any such stingy giving."

"Well, jest go ahead, I ain't partic'lar," the old man replied, after a moment of meditation, during which Mercy had been drawing her fingers through his hair, and a smile of contentment slowly diffusing itself over his face.

"I wonder if women are such dreadful creatures after all," said she sceptically, leaning upon the back of her father's chair, and continuing to stroke his hair.

"Whar's my pipe?" suddenly asked the Captain, ignoring her query.

She filled it and brought it to him and resumed her position, while the skipper lay smiling indulgently, occasionally rubbing his chin.

"Don't you smoke?" said Mercy to Algie.

"Oh, yes," he replied, producing a cigarette.

"Well, go ahead," said the Captain, "we ain't got no objections."

So the two men puffed away in the twilight, while Mercy continued to stroke her father's hair until Antonio came in to air the room and lay the table for dinner.

"Fetch her out, Tony," said the Captain briefly, and Antonio set a little table alongside of him, and placed the decanter and tumblers upon it.

"Ain't you got no water for the young man? He's young, Tony, he don't want nothin' hot."

A moment later, Tony fetched a large brown stone jug of water. "Say when!" exclaimed the Captain, pausing in uncertainty over the fifth glass.

"Oh, very little for me," said Algie.

"Well, I ain't a-goin' to press you, you kin bet your bottom dollar on that." So the skipper poured into the fifth glass what he considered a homœopathic quantity of gin, and an allopathic dilution of water, just as he would have mixed them for a child.

"Here's luck to our picture," said Algie.

"And to the very fust woman you kin find, what can't git her own way!"

Algie smiled and drank, and slightly nodded to Mercy, who was looking on.

"Now, Tony, say it's luck," said the skipper affably, pointing downwards.

Antonio was disappearing with the three tumblers, when Mercy reminded him that Mr. Abercrombie had not yet been shown his room.

CHAPTER IX.

THE chamber was large and square. A warm fire glowed upon the hearth, and Algie, left to himself, stood before it, meditating upon the simplicity of the people amongst whom he had been thrown.

After a while he turned and looked about him at the quaint old furniture. One thing which surprised him was, that, throughout the house, in unexpected places, there appeared strong touches of original artistic decoration. In this room it was most apparent.

A great four-posted bedstead supported a huge feather-bed. At the foot of this structure was a flight of steps covered with a carpet of crimson velvet. The bed was flounced around with a petticoat of Nile-green cambric, over which a netted fringe fell to the floor, with bunchy little tassels, tipping in a row, like a procession of dolls. A similar netting fell from the tester, over long green curtains, tied back to the posts with huge red bows. The great fluffy pillows had no vulgar cover of shams, but were meant to be slept upon, and promised dreamless and comforting sleep.

The floor was covered with a red carpet, thick and soft, which glowed in the firelight. Algie, loving the pleasantness of the dim light, had extinguished the candles and yielded to the sense of repose which was due to the warmth and softness of his surroundings.

He became so lost in thought, that it did not seem five minutes ere Antonio knocked gently at the door and called him to dinner.

When he descended to the dining-room, Aunt Polly was waiting, stiff and prim. Mercy came in smiling. Her face took on wonderful changes. To-night the expression was of bright and intense intelligence, and it seemed to Algie that the radiance of her countenance shone upon him when the features were making no impression. She had more color than usual, which increased the brightness of her eyes ; and her hair, brushed a little to one side, added to her intellectual appearance.

" How shall I ever paint her ? " thought he, regarding her with critical admiration. "She is not beautiful, but so varying, that I have not seen her twice the same."

" What a very pleasant room you have given me ! " said he to Aunt Polly.

" You must remember what you dream to-night," said Mercy mysteriously. " You know this is Friday, and whatever you dream in a strange place on Friday night always comes true. Be sure you keep half your senses awake to remember what the other

half dreams ; because in the morning I shall
require you to render an account of your
stewardship."

"Oh, that's cruel," said Algie. "I enjoyed so much the thought, this bleak night,
of sleeping in a feather-bed ! Who ever
dreamed in one ? They always carry me
back to the country inns in England. I remember particularly the old Shakespeare Inn
at Stratford-on-Avon, how I sank into something like oblivion in that feather-bed ! "

"No, I'm inexorable ; there must be no
oblivion this time. All the properties in that
room are mine. They were left me by my
godmother, and I demand toll out of everybody's dreams," replied Mercy impressively.

"You ought to write them in a book," said
Algie, "they would be better reading than
ghost stories."

"I reckon they would, young man, ef all
the folks was as fond o' lobster salad ez you
is ! " interposed the Captain, helping himself
abundantly for the third time.

"At all events, remember I'm not joking,"
said Mercy, quite seriously.

"Are you superstitious ? " asked Algie.

"No, I think not, but when my godmother
first left me those things I dreamed a very
strange dream, which was repeated in all its
details night after night, until I abandoned the
room, because it was so uncanny I attributed
it to reading Voltaire's *L'Inconnu*. This is
Friday. Your dream will come true ! "

8

The girl became more and more strange to him.

How on earth had she come to be reading Voltaire, and who had taught her French? He looked at her inquiringly.

"Are you wondering if I am humbugging you? No; I never, even in fun, say things I don't mean," said Mercy.

"No," replied Algie, "I was wondering who put you in the way of reading French, when you say you have lived here always."

"Oh, is that all?" she answered, with a smile of amusement. "Since I know how to read English, with the help of a dictionary and grammar, I can learn to read any language. One winter, I learned a French grammar by heart, and wrote all the exercises; and the next summer I read six or seven French books, and by the time I had finished that task, I knew so many words and idioms I scarcely needed a dictionary at all. That's simple enough, isn't it? Now I'm studying Italian on the same plan, and next year I mean to tackle German, and, although I don't know a sound, I can read and write anything I want to, and I shall feel quite prepared to take father and Aunt Polly in my arms and fly all over the world with them! You needn't laugh; much stranger things have happened!"

Algie was not laughing to ridicule the girl. Her Quixotic perseverance seemed anomalous to him, and he smiled at her enthusiasm.

" Is that the way you amuse yourself here when you get storm-bound ? " he said.

" Yes ; I like reading, I get so tired of myself."

" It's nothing but selfishness, all said and done," exclaimed Aunt Polly severely. " You're either buried in a book, or building castles on a knitting-needle, or wandering about the beaches as if you were possessed ! "

" Do you think so, really, Aunt Polly ? " asked Mercy, distressed.

" Of course I do. The first thing you know, you'll be talking to yourself, like old Granny Gooch ! "

Mercy's brow clouded.

" Do ye mean to say my child's like old Betsy Gooch ? " demanded the Captain aggressively, peering round the caster at Aunt Polly, that useful article being placed in the centre of the table and forming a screen between them.

" I said she was so absent-minded, she'd soon be like Granny Gooch, and wander about talking to herself."

" Mercy, my gal," said the Captain, looking at her inquiringly over his spectacles, " when ye ain't got nobody to talk to, jes ye come to yer old daddy ef you're lonesome like. He's allus ready to entertain ye; there ain't no use a-wastin' time a-talkin' to yerself."

Mercy looked lovingly at her father, who had evidently been so interested in a pudding that he had not quite caught the drift of the conversation.

When dinner was over they all turned round to the fire. The Captain smoked his pipe in silence, and Algie lighted one cigarette with another. Mercy resumed her eternal knitting. Such Algie thought it.

Aunt Polly, overlooking the morning's paper, very soon began sneezing and coughing, until the Captain turned upon her with a sardonic smile, saying,—

"Just make the most of it, Polly ; we're goin' to fix up a stoody ter-morrow for ourselves, and after that I don't reckon we'll have no more 'casion to trouble ye a-smokin' in here."

Aunt Polly allowed a faint quiver of derision to pass over her lips, and then left the room, sneezing violently.

All said "Good-night" very early, Algie leaving the Captain at the foot of the stairs ; but for some minutes longer he could hear him blustering about, shouting to the men below to "Outen them lights," to which came the nautical reply, "Aye, aye, sir." Then he talked a little to Sailor, who had come upstairs to prowl around, and woke the parrot from a nap on its tin bar. The bird's screams so exasperated the dog that he barked violently, and Bill Junk cursed the parrot, and the Captain swore at the whole lot, until, finally, the lights were put out, and everything became silent, save for the sounds of the Captain stumbling up the stairs in the dark, with his shoes in his hand, to prove to himself that he was as still as death.

Algie, having made himself ready for bed, blew out the candle and sat down in the arm-chair before the fire.

Mercy's dream recurred to him, and he looked at the bed with a little misgiving. At length he smiled at the absurdity of such superstition.

" As if a comfortable old bed could make people dream dreams ! " he ejaculated.

He was luxuriously clad in pajamas of India silk, and, feeling too inert to go to bed, stretched his feet toward the fire, and mused.

A screen stood before the washstand, which might have been Mercy's work, and was cov-ered with pictures and verses gathered ap-parently at random. One verse, pasted in a corner, had attracted his attention. It was familiar enough, but now its meaning was more significant to him. There was plainly an untrodden spot in Algie's heart which was opening to an unexpected guest.

> " She doeth little kindnesses,
>   Which most leave undone, or despise ;
>   For naught that sets one heart at ease,
>   And giveth happiness or peace,
>   Is low esteemèd in her eyes."
>   LOWELL.

This quality, as he saw it embodied in Mercy's character, made Algie pause to re-flect ere he blindly wandered into what he would have ordinarily considered a passing flirtation. " She's too deeply in earnest in all she feels and does ! " he murmured.

He represented to himself sophistically that he was there for business only ; but he admitted the propriety of being very cautious.

" No, she's too good for any trifling," he repeated virtuously, again and again, until at last, feeling in a particularly self-denying and peaceful frame of mind, he went to bed.

There was certainly something peculiar in the room ; but it was a pleasant peculiarity. The fine linen sheets, as light as silk, smelled of withered rose leaves, and carried him back to the sunny gardens of Adrianople. Sunk in the downy depths of the feather-bed, listening to the bleak wind whistling outside, Algie enjoyed the consciousness of his own snug comfort within, until, weary with listening, he fell so soundly asleep that even the noise which the Captain made stalking downstairs in the morning did not awaken him ; and there were long gleams of light, making stripes across the curtains, ere he rubbed his eyes and reluctantly admitted that it was time to get up.

Lying back again upon the pillows, he remembered that he had dreamed, and it was not altogether a pleasant dream that he was bound to tell Mercy.

" You look as though you had slept well, and had not seen any ghosts," said she, at breakfast, silently admiring his deliciously fresh skin.

"I never slept better in my life," Algie replied.

"And so you dreamed no dreams for my book ? " inquired Mercy.

"Oh, yes ! I dreamed a dream like a fairy ta'e. But it won't bear telling," said he.

Aunt Polly stared at him through her glittering glasses, and Algie became so nonplussed that he turned as red as red could be.

"But you promised," said Mercy, smiling with a tender feeling of compassion as she watched the color subside from his face. There is no doubt that men who color easily have great compensation for their embarrassment in the sympathy of most women.

"I ought to have a little time to make it up with effect ! " protested Algie.

"Oh, no ! " exclaimed Mercy, "because it won't come true unless you tell it at breakfast ! "

"All right," said he, "if you give me leave to withhold all the parts I don't want to come true."

"No, no ! You're much too mysterious already ! "

"But I really must think it over," persisted Algie seriously, proceeding to butter the toast which he had taken from the rack, and continuing to talk while he did so. "You know we are supposed to be in a great hurry this morning to go to work on the studio. We need a cloth hanging for the background. Could we manage to get a piece of blue denim anywhere near ? But that is so cold ; say dark-red canton flannel."

" We might, in the village ; there are shops there."

"Could *we* get it ? " inquired Algie, immediately grasping at a possibility. " Could *we* find the way ? "

" How do you mean ? " Mercy asked. " It is much too far to walk."

" No ; I mean, could we go in the gig, you and I ? " Algie blushed at his own temerity.

" I never should have thought of anything so funny ! You and I, jogging across the sands in father's old gig ! "

"Suppose it is funny ; does that make it impracticable ? You see only I could get it, because no one else would understand the style of thing, and I shall need you to go and show me the way."

"Splugen might do so," said Aunt Polly satirically.

" I'll ask father," said Mercy, smiling at Algie's evident terror of Aunt Polly.

" You know we ought to be very industrious to-day," said he, as she was leaving the room. In a few moments there was a tumult below.

Nothing gave the Captain such complete satisfaction as a "jolly good row."

Presently Algie heard him exclaim : " You know I ain't got no 'pinions in this here house ! More like than not she'll break your neck. But jest have yer own way ; I ain't a-goin' to cross ye ! "

Some protest and demur followed from Mercy, then the Captain's loud voice was heard shouting from the stable : "Confound that gal ! You know I ain't a-keerin' fur the horse, or the vehicle, but I'm more'n certain she'll break yer neck."

"Why, father, you know old Jim's so slow his bones creak in the joints," was Mercy's answer.

"At last!" cried she, rushing into the breakfast-room, brimful of smiles. "Again I've 'stooped to conquer.'"

After much more terrific ado, Algie and Mercy, each with a foot-stove, a great bear-skin rug, and innumerable precautions, set off at a funereal crawl to traverse the bleak waste of sand which lay between them and the village on the railway, where a stock of dry goods was boasted rather than displayed.

"You must tell me your dream now," said Mercy, after they had jogged along some time in silence.

"Do you really hold me to it, and promise not to be angry ?" said he.

"Angry about a dream?" said Mercy. "What a goose you must think I am !"

"Because I dreamed about you," said Algie. Mercy colored and looked away. "I dreamed," said he, encouraged, "that we—that is, you and I—went wandering in a beautiful garden, down a long and pleasant path together ; and every flower of the spring opened in succession as we passed it, until we came

to innumerable roses, sweet and delicious like
the roses at Booja ; and they were so tempting
that I gathered them for you until they spilled
out of your arms upon the ground.   And as
we continued walking, we came to a place
where the way divided into two ways, and I
wished to go on with you ; but a power beyond
my control forced me to take the other road.
I was very reluctant, but I left you with the
roses in your arms.   As we parted, you gave
me one.   A little tear fell upon it as you gave
it me, and there seemed to be a charm in the
tear.   See how foolish my dream was ; you
would not shed a tear for me, would you ? "

"I am afraid you would very quickly dash it
to the ground if I did.   Men don't like tears,"
replied Mercy, " but go on with your dream."

" Must I tell you the rest ? "said Algie ; " *do*
you exact it ? "

" Of course," said Mercy.

" Well, as I went on my separate way, to
my surprise, the flower did not wither as all
other flowers do in my hands ; for the little tear-
drop, which still lay in the heart of it, kept it
alive.   Time and again, I turned to look at
you across the garden, as you went your own
straight way ; until, finally, I became impressed
that I was going a long and lonely distance to
no purpose ; for my eyes and thoughts were
ever turning back to consider you ; and after
a while I saw that some one had joined you
and was walking in my place by your side ;
and then I turned, and tried to go back and

overtake you. It was a much longer way
than I had thought, and I was utterly wretched.
I wanted to be in that man's place ; but it was
too late, and so, all out of heart, I sat down
beside the garden path. Night was coming
on. I could still see your two figures outlined
against the blood-red evening sky, and I
sprang up, feeling determined that I would
die trying to reach you."

"And did you ?" said Mercy, eager to hear
the end of the story, and forgetful that she was
the heroine.

"Do you wish I had ?" said Algie, smiling,
and suddenly turning to look at her.

Something in his scrutiny made Mercy
tremble and drop her eyes without replying.

"No," said Algie, after a pause, and in an
altered tone, "I had not reached you when I
awoke, but I had gathered again many of the
flowers which had fallen from your arms ; and
when I had kissed them with delight at touching once again something you had touched,
they came to life in my hands, and, who
knows, if the sun had not shone in my eyes, I
might have toiled on over the hill, and have
overtaken you."

Then they were both silent for a long time,
until Mercy made an effort and said, "How
absurd dreams are !"

"Shall you write a book of dreams, and
begin with mine ?" he asked.

"Oh, no," said Mercy under her breath.

"Why not ?"

"Because I could not bear to have any one know you had dreamed that!"

"Are you sorry *you* know it?"

"No," said Mercy shamefacedly, but trying very hard to be truthful.

"Good heavens!" thought Algie, with a faint sigh of contrition, "what deep water I'm getting into! But then," he told himself, "it was the fault of that stupid old horse; he was so slow one had to talk to get rid of time!"

Algie remained silent, reflecting on what he had done. There was something true and loyal in him, even though he had spent his life for the most part frivolously. Hitherto he had known that he was trifling with triflers, and he was too generous, realizing as he did his monetary perplexities, to wish to act, even upon a fickle sincerity, with Mercy. He was suddenly brought, by the story of his dream, to look upon a possible, even probable state of things, which might await them in the future; and he experienced a noble desire to protect her, in her innocence, from any pain, even of his own making. Why had he not invented a dream? He had told much worse lies before.

But as a policy, in the long run, honesty is much the best; and should a part of the dream be realized, and Algie knew very well it would be, perhaps it would prove a superstitious solace to believe the rest might be; and as he took that comfort to his soul, his face quickly cleared.

CHAPTER X

S soon as they returned they set to work with a will, stirring up such clouds of dust that Mercy began to sneeze with a vigor that rivalled Aunt Polly's.

When that lady put her head in at the door, the Captain informed her that he detested sneezing women, and that two at once were more than he could stand.

Bill Junk's curiosity brought him up from below ; Antonio, with his child-like Neapolitan smile, also came to proffer his services. Splugen appeared with the parrot, which was more gossipy and abusive than ever ; and Sailor, in his excitement, invented new and intricate ways of getting under people's feet. But everybody was in a good humor except Aunt Polly.

The look of care was gone from Mercy's face, and she was brisk and full of life.

Before long the Captain had had enough of it, and retired to his old haunts.

Finding themselves deserted, Mercy wished to recall Splugen, but Algie had a mind that

two was company and three a crowd, and
preferred the company.

"No," cried he excitedly, embracing the
step-ladder, and rushing across the room with
it, "let's do it ourselves."

So Mercy stood at the foot of the ladder,
handing up tacks to him, and a wonderful
amount of waiting on he required, every time
just managing to touch the tips of her rosy
fingers, and steal a glance into her confiding
eyes.

When it was time for lunch, and Antonio
looked in to inform them of that fact, he grinned
in astonishment at the change.

Mercy, with her sleeves rolled up to the
shoulders, a big striped apron on, and her
arms akimbo, was a pretty enough picture,
and Algie, resting upon the step-ladder to
survey the work, looked at her admiringly.

They ate their lunch in the most undignified
haste, scandalizing Aunt Polly, and returned
eagerly to their work. It was good so far.
They had put wide bands of indigo, dark red,
old-gold, and green around the room, covering
the walls down to the oak wainscoting, which
was good and real, with its solid nail heads,
put in for a purpose, showing at every joint.

"Now you help me to drape this long silk
fishing-net over these bands of color," said
Algie, climbing up the ladder with one end of
the net; "and hand me the brass-headed
nails, one at a time, and I will drive them
wherever I can find the studding."

The net must have been fifty yards long and ten feet wide, with outlandish cork floats, which projected at intervals from the walls.

"This net carries me back so, to one night on the Bay of Naples," said Algie. "We were not allowed to land till morning—I was only a boy then—and I became so excited, running from the deck to the bridge, watching the fishing-boats come out with flaming fires in copper braziers, and the boatmen paying out the net, and these great things bobbing about so whimsically in the moonlight! A white stream of light from the moon and a red stream from the fire made it a scene I shall never forget. And another time, driving along the road from Castellamare to Pompeii, we stopped and I got out of the carriage to feel the nets; I could scarcely believe they were silk. They looked like brown cobwebs hanging from one fig-tree to another, drying in the sun. How little I thought, then, that the next time I touched one, after ten years, I should be here with you. It seems strange that I did not know you were in the world then."

"And ten years from now, I wonder where we'll be," said Mercy.

"Oh, nothing ahead of this day and hour!" cried Algie impatiently, as if he hated all beyond the present. "Now, isn't that beautiful?" said he, screwing up his right eye very unbecomingly and cocking his head on one side to get the effect. "The tone of that net is lovely!" he exclaimed, after an ecstatic pause.

"And here is another net, a blue one. What can we do with that?" said Mercy.

"Oh, stretch it like a cobweb over the ceiling." Then Algie got together a few boards to make shelves, and banged, and sawed, and hammered until he made such a racket that the whole family collected again. Upon the shelves they arranged hundreds of shells, rosy and shining, black, white, and brown, from all the seas and oceans. There were Bahama tortoise-shells polished exquisitely, a harvest of seaweed, and all kinds of dried and shrivelled things, which it made one shudder to touch. Then they sat down to rest.

"That Chinese idol must loaf in a corner, he's much too fat and lazy for a god, and the junk sail shall darken the cross light; and we'll hang the Egyptian scarfs upon the mantelpiece."

The easel which Algie had brought down from town was set in place, an Alcaldi saddle-cloth spread under it, and a Mexican blanket of the old artistic lozenge-pattern hung over it. Mercy observed that what were generally considered the off-hand effects were always the ones which cost the most pains. And then they congratulated themselves as quite successful, and sat down again before the fire, in the gathering gloom of the evening.

The girl's face was tenderly lighted by the firelight as she fell into one of her long meditations, and Algie watched her in silence. She was so quaint and original that he was constantly watching her, as if she perplexed him. What were the maidenly fancies preoccupying so innocent a mind ? Thinking ! Perpetually thinking ! He felt withal a kind of conscious wickedness that he had never felt before ; he dared not allow himself to be so happy with her. How could he, in honor, when he had never known a New Year find him rich enough to make ends meet ? What right had he to take the risk of inflicting the chances of his harum-scarum life upon her ? He had been well taught the old maxim, "When Poverty comes in at the door, Love flies out at the window." Yet he sat silently picturing to himself, in his eager susceptible way, how happy he could be with her, for he felt such satisfaction after this, their first day's work together, that he thought he should be as happy as that every day.

But Mercy, he saw plainly enough, did not know what it meant to struggle to make ends meet. She had always had her father's fortune at her command, free to give to all according to the dictates of her generous heart. Never having been tempted by a thousand idle ways of wasting money, she would not understand his difficulties if he told them. At the same time, she was the sort of woman to tempt a man's confidence.

9

He began to wish he had never come to
Cassandra Bay; never wandered on the beach
that day; never seen Mercy! It seemed ages
and ages ago to him. In reality, that was
Saturday night, and he had been there since
Wednesday. In his headlong haste he had
lived a whole lifetime in those four days.

The Captain put a stop to their reflections
by thrusting his head in at the door, telling
them dinner was coming on to the table; and
they hurried to their rooms to dress.

But Algie, notwithstanding the abstinence
of his resolves, could not resist touching
Mercy's hand, either by contrivance or acci-
dent, as, in the dusk of the room, he moved
past her to open the door.

Then his conscience smote him as he walked
up the stairs, and told him to go home. It
was a conscience which talked a great deal
and acted very little; and was most vehement
when out of temptation. But he was only
twenty-six—the prime age when the heart is
most full and eager to be happy. Moreover,
seeing that Mercy was so anxious about the
ship, he did not apprehend any unhappiness
to others, and redoubled his efforts to please
the family; his conscience to the contrary
notwithstanding. Even Aunt Polly yielded,
and admired him.

The next day was Sunday, and a heavy
gale was blowing. Mercy appeared with her
jacket buttoned up to the chin.

"Where can you be off to?" said Algie,

looking up. "You had much better get a book and keep me company."

"And leave the little boys and girls to grief?"

"What do you mean? Where are you really going?"

"About half a mile across the sands, to where a half-dozen huts shelter several dozen children whom I regale on Sundays with stories of a religious nature."

"Am I too grown-up to go? I adore stories."

"I'm afraid you are," said Mercy, abashed. "I could not possibly interest you."

"You can only prove that by turning my mind inside out. Won't you let me go?"

She could scarcely have declined if she had wished, so when he had donned a pilot jacket and a shaggy "Tam O'Shanter," he took the little basket which she had been holding in her hand, and they started across the salt marsh by a path which led over the crest of a sand cliff, and descended abruptly to the beach.

A clamor of voices arose at sight of them, and a few half-savage children gathered about the cabin toward which Mercy conducted Algie. An old man, crouching beside the door, removed a pipe from his lips to greet them. Inside, a woman having a baby at her breast dusted a chair with her apron, and invited Algie to take a seat, indicating another for Mercy.

" The wind were a-blowin' that bad I
'lowed like as not ye wouldn't be a-comin'.
I heard you'uns had company folks a-stayin'
with ye," said she, dragging up a chest to
the corner of the fire to sit upon. " I ain't a
feelin' so mighty well myself. The baby, he's
been that bad the whole night I like to not
got no sleep; but 'pears like he's a little grain
easier now."

As she spoke, she laid the child across her
knees, so that the head, suspended by a limp
little neck to a meagre body, hung over her
leg like a bag of beans.

Mercy leaned forward in painful concern
for the child. " Oh ! do let me hold him,"
she said. " I know you must be worn out.
Poor little thing !" she added, sliding her
hand gently under it, and pillowing its head
in the hollow of her arm. It was not the
freshest baby in the world, and Algie was
rather disgusted that Mercy should put her
hands on it.

The child whimpered, but the woman,
straightening herself with a sigh of relief,
poured out a panful of boiling water, and
proceeded to wash the litter of cups and
saucers which covered the table.

" You must be so uncomfortable here,"
whispered Mercy to Algie. " Don't feel
obliged to wait for me. You know I'm quite
used to it."

He shook his head negatively.

Meantime, the children began squabbling

and shoving each other against the door,
which finally burst open ; and about twenty
of them, in all stages of dishevelment,
crowded in, and huddled together upon the
floor behind Mercy's chair, fixing their eyes
upon Algie with a uniform and unbroken
stare.

" I wonder if you'll ever understand the
verse I teach you so often," said Mercy, with
a sigh of despair. " *He that hath clean
hands and a pure heart.*" Continuing to
sway the baby upon her knees, she took
from her basket a copy of " The Pilgrim's
Progress," and resumed the reading of the
story where she had left off the last time ;
occasionally pausing to inquire if they understood her.

Presently the baby set up a piping wail,
and Mercy, fearing they might disturb the
little creature, bade them follow her to a
sheltered nook outside, where they found
seats upon a wreck. All repeated the creed
and Ten Commandments with her, and afterwards they said the Lord's Prayer together,
kneeling upon the sand.

The children spoke as if they really believed that they had a God and a Father, who
would grant them their daily bread if they
asked for it. The faith which Mercy had
taught them went home to Algie.

"Who works for others, works for himself," he said sceptically, but his conscience
told him that Mercy really enjoyed the act of

doing good for those who could never do anything for her in return.

When she had finished with the children
Algie left the wreck and walked about the
beach, watching her go from door to door.
By the time her basket was empty the gale
had subsided, and the blue sky was out in
patches.

The water was gone from the pier, and
fishing-smacks lay tilted on the sand, their
gaffs dropped low, and fish-nets hung from
mast to mast.

Algie and Mercy walked along the beach,
facing Mother Margery's cabin, and were
close upon the spot where they had first met.

She so thoroughly satisfied his peculiar requirements that it seemed impossible to him
that he could have known her for so short a
time, but he felt as if in his innermost consciousness he had held her always.

The scene had changed much since that
day. Then, the tide was in, and the sea tu-
multuous after the night's storm ; now, for a
long way out, the beach was dry, and two
cliffs held the harbor bar, like a rusty chain,
over which the tide was lapping.

" I shall never forget this spot," said Algie.
" Some day, when you are not expecting me,
or have forgotten me, you may meet me here.
Do you ever feel a queer desire to repeat
yourself, to do again, perhaps with the hope
of doing better, something which you have
done before ? "

"No, never," said Mercy, "the days are too full, I have no time! But," she added laughing, "my days are all repetitions one of another. I sometimes wonder if I could endure life away from here; I don't think I could for long!"

"Wouldn't you gradually forget?"

"No, no," said Mercy, "when I go away, I am hopelessly homesick until I get back. Even when father goes with me, I miss Jack so. I am so fond of him."

"You *were* so fond of him," said Algie. He repented his cruelty in a moment; but it made him so frantically jealous, wandering in these haunts, to be forever reminded that Jack had such advantage of him.

"Jack will never be past and gone to me," said Mercy, with a quaver in her voice which cut Algie to the quick.

"You will forget your grief in time; every one forgets," said Algie, with the assurance of a man of the world.

"Forget!" cried Mercy. "Can my own life ever cease to be real to me? Could I forget you, or this moment?"

Algie winced. He could not decide whether her words were satirical; but Mercy was thinking of abstract conditions. "The past is just as necessary as the present," said she. "If we had no past, how could we exist morally or physically? If Jack's influence had not made in me some of those qualities which are integral parts of me, how could I be what

I am ; and, being what I am, how could I forget Jack ? So, also, I know I help Jack."

" Do you think you have no power to help any save Jack ? Can't you conceive that your faith in Jack is helping to make my faith in you, and, through you, in human nature at large ? Or do you care nothing about it ? Perhaps you love Jack because you can patronize him !"

His tone was so sarcastic that Mercy looked at him in wonder.

" How could I presume to patronize Jack, who is so much nobler and more generous than I am !" she exclaimed.

Moved by an impulse he scarcely understood, Algie replied.

" Is he refined and cultivated ? Is a woman capable of fully loving, or admiring with endurance, a person who commands her moral esteem only, and for whom, in all other respects, she must make apology ? I think you are in grave error. Men who are only morally superlative end by being insufferable bigots, and, in the long run, are detestable !"

" What if I thought that a man, so misjudging another who was absent, might be more detestable !" exclaimed Mercy, with her father's hot temper flashing in her eyes.

" Oh, forgive me," cried Algie, instantly recalled to himself, " I don't know why I said it ! You will forgive me, won't you ? " With heedless impetuosity he seized her hand and held it until their eyes met.

She did not know what to think of him, nor did he of himself.

"Jack will always be Jack to me," she finally said, "nor will any one ever take his dear place."

Through Algie's mind flashed a hope that Jack was done with ; but he was neither brutal nor base, and a moment later he felt that he deserved to be kicked, and said very earnestly, "Would you mind telling me what place he holds ? "

Mercy hesitated, but the moral compulsion of Algie's scrutiny compelled her to speak. " I hardly know," said she, at length, "but when I read the story of a hero of old, I can always put Jack in his place. There is no act of self-abnegation, self-immolation, even, which Jack could not achieve, if he felt that it was necessary and right. Nothing he would shrink from, even to the helping of the last old sailor to the last seat in the lifeboat and going down alone on a swamping deck. Could you, who perhaps are no such ' bigot,' do that ? "

"No, I certainly could not, and I doubt if the unidealized Jack of flesh and blood could, either, although your fisher-folk are bred to courage as a Jersey cow is bred to cream."

Mercy looked at him in contempt ; but he continued, although he turned very red, " Such courage can only be due to a lack of appreci-ation of the value of life, and to the absence of such acquirements as make a man's life essential to his fellow-beings. For example, a great singer, or sculptor, or genius of any sort, whose whole youth must be spent in acquiring an art, can't afford to die ; he owes it to that art to live. He is just as heroic when he is starving in a garret, toiling to make himself perfect, as another who only suffers once and finishes the struggle. The two ideals are different."

" Yes," said Mercy, " but your ideal sacrifices himself to an art which repays him in this world. He lives to feel the laurels on his brow ; but my ideal sacrifices himself for his fellow-men, and can have no possible reward except in immortality. He must display the sublimest courage as well as the sublimest faith. It is his soul which acts in him, believing in its own immortality. Jack's heroism could only be made perfect in death, and receive its reward in a future state, while your hero's is only a sordid endurance receiving its recompense in clapping of hands and stamping of feet. The only reward worthy of the hero whom I admire is the smile of the eternal God."

" That is just the opposite to what I think," asserted Abercrombie. " There can be no danger nor death in an immortal state, therefore Jack's courage perishes with him. Perhaps you may call my hero a fanatic. Which would you think the more practical—yours or mine ? "

"I think," replied Mercy, "that for the repose of every-day life, neither would be necessarily agreeable."

"You will admit, then," said Algie, "that
the material for every-day life is best when
not made up of apotheosized Greek heroes,
nor fanatical geniuses, but of the lukewarm
mixture which the civilization of to-day dubs
'a gentleman,' or that adaptation of incon-
spicuous qualities which in the sum of our
philosophy is called the commonplace man,—
a creature redounding with common sense!"

"It strikes me there is not much common
sense in this conversation of ours, for I have
begun to think you have been trying to con-
vince me that a gentleman cannot be a hero,"
said Mercy.

"Not by any means. Occasionally they
happen to be ; but, rather, that heroes are
not commonly gentlemen. Achilles was a
hero, but, measured by the standard of to-day,
he was no gentleman to drag old Hector in
the dust ; on the contrary, I think he was an
abnormal beast, and deserved to be pounded
with the butt-end of a thunderbolt."

"Oh, Mr. Abercrombie, how can you be so
irreverent!" cried Mercy in dismay.

"I'm not irreverent," protested Algie; "they
were savages, and I pretend to be a gentleman."

"Do you mean to imply that all heroes are
savages?" demanded Mercy indignantly.

"Well, yes, if you will have it. It's the

triumph of savage nerve, which has not been weakened by sentiment, over intellectual economy.   In early days men, for lack of revelation, adored beasts, and the more brutal a man was, the more blood he could wade through, the more god they thought him.   In the middle ages men adored mystical revelation, in these days they adore brains!"

Mercy shook her head doubtfully, and Algie resumed:

"Else why do you study so hard when you are alone?   It is the inherent desire of your nature to approach the ideal which it adores.   Show me a man's god, and I will show you the man, because he will inevitably try to make himself like his deity, or his deity like himself.   You will outlive the heroic ideal, as your intellectual desires become stronger.   You will outgrow Jack, just as Jack will outgrow himself—for old men are seldom heroes.   Their courage changes into magnanimity."

"Do you know," said Mercy, looking at him inquiringly, "I feel as if you had led me into a comparison between Jack and yourself. I don't agree with you.   If old men are seldom heroes, it is because they have become cowards through experience, and trust their judgment to arbitrate where they know they would be beaten.   It only proves to me that old age is less noble than youth."

Abercrombie, startled by her remark, had turned crimson, convinced of its truth, whilst she, feeling that she had been too pointed, blushed for herself.

Blushing and confused, they looked at each other, until Mercy, recovering herself, said abruptly,—

" I won't grant any of your arguments, except upon circumstantial evidence."

" All right ! " said Algie, offering his hand ; " but will you promise, fair and true, that if I ever should ask you for your conclusions, based upon such evidence, you will give them to me without evasion ? "

" Upon condition," replied Mercy, " that you also promise me that when it is proven to you that you are wrong, as it surely will be, you will own up. My premises are, that intrepidity is consistent with gentleness, and that the power to lay down one's life and die for a simple human end may coexist with mental ambition as well as common sense."

" Yes," responded he, " but always assuming that it be done in the necessary carrying out of the demands of every-day life, and upon no romantic, uncalled-for, or eccentric adventure."

" Very well, I'll shake hands upon it. It's a bargain, and we'll find our proofs," said Mercy, accepting Abercrombie's hand, and little dreaming of how it should be proven.

CHAPTER XI.

ERCY was a shrewd observer, and wondered if Algie really thought all he had said. He colored under her scrutiny and beat the fluted sands with his stick, feeling that he had been guilty of a mean act in endeavoring to undervalue Jack's courage. He knew very well that if the hero had been any other than Jack, he would have been much less deprecatory, for, in his secret heart, he fostered a good deal of hero-worship.

He began to fear that Mercy might think less of him because of it. How could she make allowance for this aversion to an unknown man which had arisen in his breast?

He felt detestable, knowing that he had been decrying the very element of dauntless courage which was the backbone of Mercy's own character, and which, combined with her intelligence and originality, made her so fascinating to himself; and, glancing askance at the gentle face, he admitted that she combined many of the attributes of Minerva with the most feminine tenderness.

"I believe you doubt me after all," said he.

"I do. Perhaps you are braver than you think," she answered.

"Do not make any such false estimate of me," he replied earnestly. "I would rather you thought less of me than I deserved, than more. I could not bear to be spurious to you, of all people in the world."

Algie thought he was speaking truth, for he felt morally certain that if he had one spark of heroism, he would fly Cassandra and this delicious dallying. He asked himself what was to be the end of it.

How could he tie his arrogant family, fastidious even among cultivated people, to this clan of rough fisher-folk, which reminded him of a great oyster bed—ugly, wholesome, and nutritious, producing this one pearl? It seemed madness altogether, for he knew that the pearl could only be removed with the death of the oyster.

Abercrombie was ignorant that the Captain's dominant ambition was that Mercy should be a lady. Dearly as he loved her, he would have been satisfied to yield her up and watch her from afar, believing that the ignoble bivalve was not worthy to keep the precious thing it had begotten. The pride of his whole being reached its climax in Mercy. Nothing was good enough for her. Golden hairpins and ruby rings were less than fit. It was marvellous that the girl was not cor-

rupted by such indulgence. The secret lay
in the fact that her ideal, mingling, as it did,
the transcendental with the transitory, was
far above and beyond anything which the
Captain could devise for her. She believed
in the moral exaltation which would result to
her from the endeavor to adapt herself to her
harsh surroundings, and it was that daily
self-abnegation which gave to her countenance the light of saintliness that Algie so
admired.

But the most spiritual of women could have
had no perfect power to withstand the flattery of a man whose plausible devotion had
the polish resulting from constant practice,
and whose warmth, if short-lived, was mag-
netic.

As they continued their walk, these qualities made Jack's rough and sturdy nature
seem coarse by contrast, and, upon approach-
ing the O'Doons' cabin, she shrank within
herself in a new and strange way.

But she remembered that in darkness
and danger he had proven himself to be
trusted, as his father and brothers had before
him.

Had not her own father been humbly
enough born? How was she better than
Jack, save for what money brought? She
reproached herself bitterly. Since they had
been little boy and girl together, reading
fairy tales or playing in the sand, there had
been an undefined feeling of loyalty to Jack's

rights, whatever they were, and she now demanded of herself that he should be treated with reverence worthy the hero she believed him. Mother Margery also had always been heroic to her, and there was a momentary feeling of passionate resentment toward Algie as an intruder who had come between herself and them.

When she and he reached the cabin, they found the door open to admit the sunshine. At first no one was visible, but on looking more carefully, they found the old man lying asleep upon the bed. He breathed huskily.

Mercy went and laid her hand gently upon his head. A painful apprehension came upon her. His flesh was clammy to the touch. She looked anxiously at Algie, but, being ignorant of illness, he could not interpret her expression.

"He must be very ill indeed," said she, going to the door to look out; "I am sure Mother Margery has gone for help." Then she went to the hearth, raked the coals together with the stump of a firebrand, and filled the kettle with water.

"Suppose he were to die before Jack gets back," said the girl; "his heart is almost broken."

Abercrombie was no longer capable of surprise at anything which Mercy might do or say concerning the living or the dead, and sat watching her mutely, his eyes wandering with keen artistic appreciation over the quaint

10

walls. The mind which had conceived the curious combination was closely in accord with his own.

There was such unutterable pathos in the suggestion of each shred. Even the gorgeous figure-head apologized for its degradation! Something in the mildewed sails, in the frippery of the gilded door, in the silence of the little tremulous crabs wriggling in the breeze, smote him with a pang of pity for the unknown, unguessable things of which each fragment had been a part.

Turning suddenly to Mercy, he asked her who had arranged them.

" Jack," she replied, and added, quoting his own speech of an hour before: "Show me a man's god, and I will show you the man." Then she went on : " Here, too, I have spent much of my life."

Just at that moment the old man upon the bed seemed to be strangling. He did not recognize Mercy ; not even when she lifted his head upon her shoulder.

" Pour a little coffee in the cup and bring it to me," said the girl to Abercrombie, who did so with great agitation. " Try and compose yourself," she added, seeing that his hand trembled violently. He looked at her in astonishment.

Just then a shadow fell upon them, and Mother Margery entered with the Captain.

" Take him, Mother Margery, he does not know me," said Mercy, making room for her beside the bed. The old woman lifted her husband in her arms.

"Yes," said the old man, endeavoring to follow with his eyes an imaginary object across the room, "I know'd he were a-comin'. He do look well. Extraordinary well. There ain't nar'a sich another fine boy at the fishin'." He stopped bewildered, and then put out his hand, his face alight with an ineffable smile. "He's a-comin', I know'd he war a-comin'.

His hand suddenly dropped heavily, his eyes lost their light and stared blindly before him, and his head gradually sank backwards. Those looking on expected to hear a word, a sigh, a single shuddering breath ; but there was nothing. He was dead.

Mother Margery looked on as if it were beyond belief, and then with a dreadful cry she flung herself across the body.

The Captain blew his nose and walked out, with that sudden cold in the head which he always assumed when his neighbors fell into trouble.

It seemed to Abercrombie that Mercy was made of humanized iron. She was standing beside her foster-mother, looking pityingly at her and trying to draw her away by the hand.

He had never see a man die before, and was surprised that it was not horrible. Perhaps the first thought that comes to one, on seeing a stranger die, is the wish to be in his place, that it might all be over with, since,

some day Death must come to us as well.
He wondered to see Mercy treat death so
familiarly, for after a moment the girl, with
great effort, but with method and firmness,
straightened the old man's back, laid his
arms down by his side, closed his eyes, and
then, turning to Abercrombie, touched his
sleeve and motioned him to follow her out
of the cabin. Involuntarily he felt his flesh
creep when she touched him. Her will was
so strong, and her self-command so resolute,
that he was afraid of her.

"Shall we leave your foster-mother alone?"
he asked, moving reluctantly from the door,
which he was surprised to see Mercy close
after them.

"I'm doing as I would be done by," she
answered.

Walking away toward the little hamlet they
had left but an hour before, they descried
fishermen hastening toward them. "I'm so
glad father found you, O'Reill," said Mercy;
"if you will wait outside the cabin a while,
it will be good of you. You know of old that
Mother Margery fights her battles best alone.
I'll come back after a while and take her
away."

So the fisherman went and sat down beside
the door of the cabin in the sun, and soon
others came and sat beside him, waiting, in a
kind of awe-stricken silence, until Mercy should
come back.

Meantime, she and Algie climbed the cliff

where it was shelving, and followed the path through the salt marsh. At length Mercy, observing that her companion was silent, looked at him inquiringly.

"I don't know what to make of you," said Algie abruptly.

It was wonderful what startling truths Mercy's eyes probed out of people.

"You think, perhaps, that I have no human feeling," said she in reply, as if she had read his thoughts; "but," she added after a pause, "do you really believe, that if I had no feeling, I, young as I am, could have forced myself to look at death so often and in so many dreadful shapes, as to appear to look upon it now with indifference? I have learned the necessity for absolute self-control, and that, by means of it, I can often do for others what they are too excited to do for themselves. I can't remember the day when the first dying hand was clasped in mine! They are rough people, you think," she added, after studying his face for a moment, "and one cannot do much for them; but they know they will never call upon me in vain, and more than all, they feel that they are mine, my very own. And rough, as I freely grant they are—wrangling, swearing, drunken, drowning—they all have that heroic stuff in them which you despise and I prize beyond everything. Doubtless it is the savage in me which gives me the power to endure the sight of it all. Oh, believe me, there can be no other life so hard,—no

such suffering—as upon the sea; and because
no such suffering, no such heroism ; and when
I see an old sailor die, it makes me feel such
intense sympathy for him, that I almost could
be heroic.   The grandest power of the sea is
the strength it brings out in those who suffer
at their work upon it."

As she ceased speaking, her eyes filled with
passionate tears, and she could not have said
more if she had wished ; but her breast
heaved, and it seemed to Abercrombie that
there were many thoughts she would have
uttered if she could.   Mercy covered her face.

The man saw that her nerves had been
overtaxed, but, as she approached the garden
gate, she dried her eyes.

Bill Junk was at the door, and Mercy told
him of O'Doon's death, and ordered a basket-
ful of food to be sent to the cabin.

When they were once more in the sitting-
room, the girl sank into a chair, shaking violently.

" What is it ? What is the matter ? " cried
Algie in desperation, endeavoring very gently
to take her hands from her face.

" Oh, nothing," said Mercy, " but it seems
as if I could stand all kinds of things like a
rock, until they are over, and then all of a
sudden, oh, something—I don't know what—
gets the matter with me, and I feel as if my
heart had almost stopped beating, and something hurts me so, here ! " she exclaimed,
pressing her hand on her breast.

"You are killing yourself for all these old ruffians !"

"They are mine, I should be willing to die for them."

The speech and look, although they would never have been expressed had she not been exhausted beyond control, were such exponents of Mercy's character, that Algie always remembered them. Such a passionate devotion, misguided though it often was, he had never seen. But when the excitement had subsided, her cheeks became livid, and Algie rang for Antonio. As soon as the old man saw his young mistress, he hurried to mix a "hot Scotch"; and, while the water seemed slow to boil, sat grumbling over the kettle, exasperated at Mercy's unqualified self-sacrifice.

"Look a-here, Tony," interrupted Bill Junk, "don't you be a begrudgin' ole Ned his little bit o' comfort at the las'; you knows ef 'twas you (and you may bless the Lord A'mighty it ain't) you'd a been glad to a-had her thar. The Lord'll give her her due when the payin' time comes. Jest don't you be a-grumblin' at the chances she's took to save up His favors. All yer little beads, and yer grimy little doll babies ain't equal to one live woman by a long shot. Hurry up them kettles and don't be puttin' no complaints in the way o' the Lord's doin's."

It was not often that Bill Junk was struck with even an emotional wave of religion, but when he was he managed to let it fall with a good break, on both Tony and Splugen, both of whom stood rather in awe of him.

" Here comes the old skipper now. He's a-blowin' his nose frightful," said Splugen, who was looking out of the window.

" I'll jest cook this here beefsteak about half," said Bill Junk, turning it over on the broiler, " an' they can finish it to-night. Like ez not, I'll be thar myself," for Bill dearly loved conviviality, and a " wake" was better than nothing festive at all.

The Captain ascended the stairs with a slow and ponderous tread, grunting at every step.

" Well, there ain't no more of 'em !" he said, slamming the door behind him, and stuffing his red handkerchief half way into his coat-tail pocket. " When the young ones goes, it's time the ole ones was gittin' out o' the way ; and I never yet knowed the day when ole Ned didn't do the right thing in the right place, an' darn'd quick too ! "

The Captain's manner was brusque and severe, and did not suggest the fact that, because of the tenderness of his heart, he had been wandering among the sand-hills, talking to himself, for a good half hour, and I fear the old fellow would resent it if I added that his eyes were red, as though he had been weeping.

" The Lord bless him ! " he ejaculated after a pause, during which he had been chasing his handkerchief around his legs and blowing his nose again. " I ain't never know'd no

honester man. Mercy, you'd better fetch ole
Margery up here. There's bread enough for
one more, I reckon ; an' there ain't no use of
us keepin' up two establishments like " (as if
he did not already support a dozen). "Jest
you fetch her along, and tell her I'm agreeable;
and I ain't got no objections. Not that there's
any use o' my havin' none, ef I were a min'
to. There ain't no use fur no man to have no
'pinions in this worl' ! I tell you, young man,
the day's a-comin', an' it's close on han' too,
when men's rights is got to be purtected !
Where ye gwine to now ? " interrupting himself impatiently to interrogate Mercy.

"I'm going to Mother Margery's," said
she.

" Lord, ain't you got enough of it ! It do
turn my stomick to see a woman run after
dead folks so ! Set down ! Send Splugen !
Send Tony ! Send Polly ! Let her take 'em
some of them little bits o' paper. It'll 'muse
'em like ; but do set down ! "

Just then Antonio appeared with the hot
toddy. The smell of it roused the Captain,
and he braced himself up, while Tony
"fetched her out ! "

Mercy shook her head negatively at Algie,
whose glance implored her to stay, as she
moved toward the door.

The Captain spread his handkerchief over
his knee, and proceeded in a tone of disgust :
" There ain't no use a-talkin' to her ! I ain't
no more vally than a green catapillar what

can't do more'n hatch a butterfly, and there
she be ! " crooking his thumb over his shoulder tragically, and looking at Algie for sympathy, which was given abundantly.

CHAPTER XII.

F Mercy had ever experienced any great personal sorrow, she could not have so courageously borne such a constant strain of sympathy for others. As it was, she had the ignorance and energy of youth to sustain her, and, full of the benevolence of her mission, went on her way, although with a divided heart.

Abercrombie had been so devoted that, never before having had so charming a companion, she felt for the first time how painful it was to tear herself from youth and pleasure to devote her thoughts to old age and death.

In her extreme conscientiousness, she took herself harshly to task, as she plodded along through the sand-hills, because her heart perpetually reverted to the fireside at home, where her father sat grumbling, and Algie morosely silent.

It did not occur to her that that young man would stand at the window with his hands in his pockets and a scowl upon his face, damning his luck in being left to watch her racing before the wind, and wishing he were going too, even into a graveyard or mortuary chapel, rather than being left alone.

He pulled his moustache fiercely.

Her determination, her unyouthful youth, her over-positiveness, exasperated him. "Why couldn't she stay quietly at home, and leave the O'Doons, dead or alive, to the fisher-folk now gathering like crows about that wretched hovel? But no! she must gratify her own predilections at any cost. Women of that type have very fine sentiments, but they take care never to do anything they don't want to do!"

The Captain was thinking about the same thing; but he hated solitude, and grumbled very loud, although neither man paid the slightest attention to the other.

Just then Algie caught sight of Splugen coming out of the house with a huge hamper upon his shoulder, and, rather than be alone, seized his yarn cap and rushed after him.

When they had gone but a short distance, he was exasperated at finding that his companion would talk only of Mercy's goodness. He was sick of that already, though free to grant that she nursed the sick, fed the poor, and comforted the miserable. But he was tired to death of it. He was miserable himself! Why dawdle with an old sailor and listen to his yarns?

What was Mercy? Nothing but a stubborn, goody-good little prig! He detested prigs. He preferred girls with more common sense and humanity. Saints were so self-righteous!

He got out a cigarette and a box of wax-matches ; but the wind was as outrageous as the people, and blew them out one after another.

He threw the cigarette away and stamped upon it, rubbing it into the sand with the toe of his shoe, until he felt like a fool and looked like one, walking on in angry silence.

But the fact that Mercy was not easily won from her old friends made him so much the more vehement that she should turn wholly to himself ; and notwithstanding that he had berated her, he was tenaciously thinking of her, and found himself saying : " So fond and true and companionable."

Though he had deserted Splugen, his steps trended toward the sea, until he arrived at the village, whither he had been but a few hours before in her company.

It was deserted. The cabin-doors were open or ajar. Only one house seemed inhabited. The inside of that, as regards material, was much like the O'Doons' ; but it lacked the poetry which pervaded Jack's home. An old woman was sitting beside the fire with a child at her feet.

" Come in," said she, in a querulous voice, " there ain't none o' the folks to hum. But bein' as ye're here, ye kin jest set down,"—rapping a chair with a cane she had taken from the chimney-corner.

" I suppose," said Algie graciously, " they are all gone to the O'Doons'."

"Yes, they says ole Ned is dead at las'. He have seen a sight o' tribulation in his day, not ez he didn't desarve every bit, an' more. I hearn ez Mercy, en some sort o' strange man, jes' happen'd thar in season. Like ez not you be the man?"

"Yes," said Abercrombie, chafing at her rude familiarity in calling Mercy by her Christian name.

"That Mercy be allus a-steppin' in when there ain't nara a soul a-lookin' fur her. She's sort o' like her daddy en her mammy both. Like ez not ye never seed her mammy. She died afore your time p'r'aps. Leastways Mercy never seed her herself. Them O'Doons allus war a prancin' lot. With their heads so high, they kinder b'lieve that gal b'longs to 'em. An' that Jack, a fine lad they say, but settin' up ter be a scholar! I ain't got no patience with no sech!" She stopped speaking, and, taking a clay-pipe out of her mouth, spat into the fire.

She was so rank of turpentine and tobacco that Abercrombie could scarcely endure her.

"I'm afraid the family is about wound up now," said he.

"Yes, that's my notion, but Mercy is that obstinate, 'tain't nothin' but pure contrariness, she won't believe nothin' she don't see, en' she keeps a-tellin' that ole fool Margery not to give up hopes; but it's a rare luck to hope agin sich evidence; en we uns, leastways, we sailor folks, knows well enough, the sea don't give back no dead."

She poked the fire with her stick, talking almost inarticulately with the pipe in her mouth. Then, withdrawing it, she chuckled to herself, like a hideous witch grinning at the thought of youth and hope.

" Miss Blessington is devoted to you all," said he.

" Who, Mercy? " she exclaimed scornfully.

" Yes," responded Algie, provoked.

" Yes," she repeated, " an' well she may be. How many on us is lost our young men folks, a-toilin' in her daddy's boats to make money fur him ! "

" They were making a living for themselves as well," said Algie, angry at her ingratitude. " Do you think Mercy owes you anything because her father gives your men employment, and doubtless good wages as well ? They choose their calling, and must take their chances."

" Oh, the Capting is fa'r enuff, fur all I knows to the contrary. I ain't never hearn o' his owin' no man nary a dollar. But he's that big a fool, and there ain't no fool like a ole one, his head is jes' completely turned with that gal. Not but what'n she's a fine enuff gal, I'll 'low ! There ain't bin a Sunday this whole winter, an' many's the day besides, but she's brung me a bowl o' soup, er a beefsteak, er a sassage, er somethin' like ; but

that nasty fellow, Bill Junk, I hates the groun'
he walks on. Don't never put no salt in
nothin' !   I likes things tasty ef I *were*
poor ! "

"It seems to me," said Abercrombie,
"that you ought to be thankful to her, instead of grumbling so much ; for there are not
many girls, none that I know of, who would
be willing to take so much trouble for an old
woman like you ; especially when she doesn't
get any credit for her pains."

"Oh, that's jest the way with ye rich uns.
Ye gits a sight o' money out'n us poor folks,
and then ye gits the big head, an' is so stuck
up, ye ain't got the time to spar' to be a-
thinkin' about the likes o' us.   Git out'n here,
I can't abide ye ! " she cried suddenly, waving
her cane at Algie, who backed out of the
cabin in sheer horror, and only recovered
himself when he was at some distance upon
the beach.

Had he reflected, he would have seen that
the old woman's jealousy of the O'Doons was
the cause of her spitefulness.

If Mercy could forgive her, after listening
patiently to such tirades whenever she came
within hearing, it was quite absurd that Abercrombie should be indignant, when he had
left the house on purpose to ventilate the hateful thoughts he had been thinking of her, and
which had emanated from the same cause,
namely, jealousy of the O'Doons.

But though he was quite willing, upon occasion, to abuse those whom he loved, he resented it fiercely if others did so, even in a milder degree.

When still far from Mother Margery's cabin, he saw two figures wandering on the beach, which finally disposed themselves upon a pile of wreckage. He correctly surmised that they were Mother Margery and Mercy.

Satisfied to be within sight of her, he sat down upon a spar and watched the incoming tide, with that practised habit of study which an artist acquires through his imagination, ever carrying about with him the spiritual body of a color-box.

Abercrombie began saying to the artist-soul within him, "Cobalt, rose, madder, white, and a touch of Naples yellow," mixing them upon an imaginary palette, with an imaginary knife, and trying them against the extreme distance. "Antwerp blue, raw umber, yellow ochre for the deep hollows of the waves; Indian red, and white, perhaps a very little cadmium for the shrimp-pink lights where the waves leap up and catch the sun." Then he painted away briskly, all on a visionary canvas, until at last some trifle aroused him, and he found himself robbed of his canvas, sitting with empty hands, alone upon a shining beach, watching the foam drawing a little nearer every time the waves came in.

After a while, having waited in vain for Mercy to notice him, he returned to Blessington House.

11

The Captain was still asleep in his chair; and Aunt Polly, having rigid ideas of Sabbath-keeping, was not visible.

At length, overpowered by the loneliness, he went into the studio. It was a long room and allowed a good length to walk; but his thoughts hovered about the little hut under the sand-hill.

Again and again he stopped at the window and peered out into the twilight to see if Mercy were coming.

But at last, as there was not the faintest vision of anything moving, quite out of heart, he took his cap and went below. The door which led into the room used by the three sailors as a galley was ajar. He paused upon the threshold and looked in.

"Has Miss Blessington come?" he asked.

"Lord, no, sir," said Bill Junk affably. "She ain't goin' to leave ole Margery, not her, sir."

"Can she be going to stay in that awful place all night!" he exclaimed, half aloud.

"There ain't no tellin', sir, she do pretty much what she's a mind to."

Algie went out and started along the path, which was obscure in the moonlight; but he felt as if possessed. Suddenly turning the angle of a sand-dune, he espied a dark figure hurrying toward him. He was startled, but Mercy's voice reassured him.

"Don't be afraid of me," she said; "why have you come out?"

Abercrombie grasped her hand, as if he had

not seen her in years ; he was so glad to touch her once more, after all the hard things he had been thinking about her.

"I don't know why I have come to look for you," he replied, "since I could not imagine that either my wishes or opinions would weigh with you one atom ; but it did seem so unearthly for you to stay there all night, that I might have been guilty of the folly of going to beg you to come back with me."

"I could not come before," she said, although she did not tell him how much she had wished to. "I have been trying to get Mother Margery to come home with me, but she won't come, although half the village is there to wake the dead. She feels that this is the very last one of all, and I suppose it is natural. If I were she, I should wish to be faithful, even to the grave. However, that is but a dog-like, senseless kind of fidelity, which can do no good to any one."

"I'm thankful you've come home," said he almost tenderly, and his voice sounded more gentle in the darkness. "Aren't you afraid to walk alone across these marshes ? Suppose you lost your way. There surely must be quicksand hereabout, for the tide rises and falls in the lagoons. You are reckless, I think, and I certainly should not allow it."

"Perhaps not," said Mercy, so quietly that Abercrombie fancied she was satirical.

The girl felt that it would be a great relief

to her if some one would take the burden of
her conscience, and say distinctly what she
might and what she might not do.   But instead of expressing that desire, she turned toward him and said half mockingly, "Who
made thee thy brother's keeper?"

The bantering tone belied her heart.   How
could he know that she had been reviling her
own want of humanity in wishing herself at
home with him ; and now thrust him bravely
from her, in order to protect herself from the
glamour of his fascination ?

"Every man has a right to look out for any
woman when occasion demands it ; else do
you think I should be groping among these
sand-hills, with the hope of relieving you from
a kind of self-inflicted martyrdom ?   I wonder
your father permits you to act so !"

Mercy was silent for a few moments, then
she replied with the same half-laughing voice,
"Perhaps it's a lucky thing for me that you
are not vested with my father's authority. I'm
afraid I should become quite timid !" nevertheless she thrilled with pleasure that he had
shown the desire for that authority.

Though women are often thus perverse,
their perversity is used to protect themselves,
just as men joke to divert attention from tears
they are ashamed to show.   Women hate to
have their hearts escape from their own keeping, and, to blind the inquisitive eye, will
sometimes belie their tenderest feelings.

Abercrombie was sensitive, and felt rebuffed. The path being narrow, he walked ahead ; but it widened as they approached the house, and he offered her his arm.

Mercy felt snubbed and very quiet ; he felt snubbed and quiet too. How could he know that, although her conscience was forever saddling her with some new burden, nothing short of death could ever lay aside an old one ? The more he thought of her, the more a martyr the girl seemed, and the more he fancied that he would like to be master of the situation.

The road was abominably short, although he walked as slowly as he could.

The next day Mercy persistently devoted herself to Mother Margery. The Captain was as cross as two sticks, and Aunt Polly worse than nobody, so Algie was forced to drudge at putting a sky into a picture ; working from the window, whence a fine cumulus cloud could be seen floating grandly.

In the evening he went again to meet Mercy.

" How much longer is this thing going to last ? " he inquired impatiently.

" They will bury him to-morrow and that will be the last of it," said Mercy reproachfully.

" Well, I'm glad of it," he exclaimed, with more candor than feeling. Mercy did not reply. Perhaps she thought the same.

She had reason to be weary of the strain, having played a tedious part all day, and done justice to the feeling she imitated, so that none save her own heart had known its weariness.

The next day was Tuesday. After breakfast the Captain spluttered around with more steam on than usual. The day was overcast, but he appeared in his best black broadcloth coat. A new broad-brimmed silk hat was in his hand, and, when not otherwise engaged, he took his handkerchief and twirled it flightily around the crown, and held the hat to catch the light.

He was altogether brand new from top to toe. Even his shoes had an extra shine, and he had taken care to provide himself against contingencies, with two handkerchiefs, one in each coat-tail pocket.

Aunt Polly presently appeared in a rustling black silk gown. She wore an old-fashioned black bonnet, very flat on top and very full over the ears, to which was attached a love veil.

Mercy went about her affairs much as usual, and at length came downstairs carrying a large prayer-book in her arms.

When they left the house, Splugen and Bill Junk accompanied them. Antonio, being a Roman Catholic, remained at home, and satisfied himself with making occasional remarks in a conciliatory tone to the image in the corner, at whose feet he was busily engaged in rubbing the household silver. Now and then he glanced in the direction of the graveyard.

The Captain and Aunt Polly walked ahead, he stepping out with imposing swagger, while she minced along, her silk dress crinkling in the light.

Algie and Mercy followed, and afterward came Splugen and Bill Junk. They could hear the parrot screaming angrily at being left behind. Sailor, suspecting that something was about to happen, had hid outside the gate, and came cringing after them.

When they reached the O'Doons' cottage, they found a goodly number already assembled—very plain folk, with rough skins and sunburnt locks. Some of the women had babies in their arms, others led young children by the hand.

All gave place to the Captain's family. Mercy, leaving Abercrombie, joined Mother Margery.

O'Doon's body had been sewed up in a hammock, and lay stretched on a rude bier.

The scene was strange to Abercrombie. It was grief without ceremony, but the tears were real.

Six men took up the bier, and started along the beach with it, and the rest of the folk fell into a double line, and followed. Some one with a nasal voice raised a droning hymn to the moan of the now ebbing tide, and all joined in the singing, keeping step to the dismal cadence.

The Captain walked beside the bier, carrying in his hand the prayer-book which Mercy had provided. He had some difficulty in getting his great silver-rimmed spectacles out of their long tin case, but having succeeded, he closed it with a snap and returned it to his pocket. Mercy having placed a conspicuous marker at the first page of the burial service, he was able to find the place. Holding the book well up before his eyes, and leaning his head very far back, he read a few paragraphs in his deepest voice, while the people left off singing to listen.

Then they sang another hymn, I had almost said another incantation—it was so droning and oracular—dying away at times to one voice. It sounded barbaric to Abercrombie.

He looked at Mercy, but she was preoccupied with Mother Margery, who walked along, staring at the passing sand.

When they had left the sea and skirted the little hamlet, they took an indefinite path across the hills, and came at last to a forlorn graveyard, enclosed by a writhing windbreak of pitch-pine and cedar. There were graves in it marked with gravestones driven by hard gusts into every attitude and covered with black lichens like hieroglyphics of woe.

One grave only bore wreaths of immortelles. The graveyard was on a high white bluff, so that the grave was deep and dry, and a box was already lowered into it.

They all stood around, while the Captain proceeded with the solemn service.

When they had finished the last sad duty

of filling the grave, the people waited for the Captain to move away, but the Captain had something to say.

"My friends," he began, after a moment's silence, during which he had blown his nose reflectively and put on his hat, "we have all come here this day to perform the last solemn duty o' layin' away our ole frien' O'Doon. He were a good frien' to all on us, to you, ez well ez to me, en while he was livin' we loved to call him Ned, 'ole Ned,' some did, not ez he were so very ole neither, seein' ez he were jes' ten year older'n me, and I am— I am—let me see! How old am I, Mercy?"

"Fifty-seven in June."

"Yes," continued the Captain with emphasis, "seein' ez I be fifty-seven in June. But when ye see his name, we'll put Edward on the tombstone, bein' ez it's more polite like; en when the likes o' ye what's growin' up to catchin' no fish at all—but livin' in idleness," glancing at the small boys, "when the likes o' ye sees the name o' Edward O'Doon on his gravestone, ye'll remember he were a man that ain't had no superior for darin' ter do whatever he were bid. I've seed him when he were a strong young man, and I were a cabin-boy, knocked ez flat ez a flounder, when a sail's a-busted, an' the ragged ole canvas had flung out a arm like, and struck him dead fur a time! He war a brave man to the backbone. An' I've seed him climb aloft when the win' war strainin' the ship-timbers that hard, it 'peared like the jib-boom war a-tryin' to swop places with the spanker. Thar wa'nt nothin' he know'd he war afeared on."

The Captain paused, and glanced contemptuously at the rabble of boys collected in a group and staring curiously at him, apparently much impressed.

" An', I guess thar ain't many o' ye'll be like him ! An' his sons, what war every one on 'em chips o' the ole block, is climbed ter the very top-gallant mast, and the Lord knows, ez I believe, they're keepin' on a-climbin' still ! "

The Captain's voice broke and, he stopped and turned away, blowing his nose, and so burying his face in his handkerchief that he did not see the short, broad, muscularly built, open-browed young man, who stood at his elbow ; but Mercy did, and uttered a cry, endeavoring to reach him, but fell at his feet insensible.

CHAPTER XIII.

 SUDDEN look of joy in the stranger's face had responded to Mercy's recognition, while the crowd, aroused by the cry as she had fallen, turned to look at the man.

Mother Margery pressed her hands upon her temples as if she were going mad ; the boys stared curiously at him, and Algie, with premonitory aversion, felt his heart sink, for the stranger was none other than Jack O'Doon, who, as if to belie the Captain's words, had appeared thus mysteriously amongst them.

"O God ! Can it be true ?" passed like a questioning prayer from Mother Margery's lips, for she doubted the evidence of her wearied senses, and drew back incredulous. But Jack, who had a full and terrible realization of the scene, leaned across Mercy's prostrate figure and touched his mother's hand, saying :

"Yes, thank God mother, it is true."

And then he stooped down and lifted the girl, who lay looking as if she were dead.

"Mercy, Mercy !" cried the Captain, shaking her roughly in his distress. But there was no appearance of life.

The crowd pressed forward breathlessly, ruthlessly trampling over the new-made grave.

Abercrombie, pale with fear and jealousy, volunteered a conjecture: "She must have fainted. Lay her down."

"No!" said Jack, glancing with weather-wise eyes at the cloud-rack beating in, ragged and black from the sea. "No!" he repeated, with the decision of a man accustomed to command, and taking Mercy up in his arms as if she had been a child, he stolidly walked away with her toward the cluster of huts.

The moment he had gained a few steps in advance of the others, he looked yearningly into the pale face against his shoulder, and heaved an anxious sigh, muttering: "My darling, my darling!"

He felt that he had been of late under an evil star, which, in default of bringing death to himself, had seen him saved out of deadly peril to find his father dead, no doubt of grief for him, and Mercy overwhelmed at his return.

He recollected that he had often seen her press her hand upon her heart as if there were pain there, and heard her say that it felt as if it were stopping.

With this sudden terror in his breast he looked at her again, clasping her closer and leaning his ear over until his cheek almost touched her lips. She was very cold, and he could not perceive her breathing.

As usual, Granny Gooch's door stood open, and Jack strode in, terrifying the old crone almost out of her wits.

She thought he was a ghost and began shrieking so wildly that she could not easily be quieted.

Her dirty bed was covered with a ragged quilt, but not seeing anything better Jack laid Mercy upon it, though he could not relinquish her head to Granny Gooch's pillow, which was soiled with snuff and smelled of turpentine and grease ; so he knelt beside her, holding her head on his arm.

"Come and see what's the matter," said he, as soon as his mother and Mercy's people had finished their slower steps to the cabin.

Aunt Polly was in a rustling fidget, while Mother Margery unbuttoned Mercy's coat and drew off her gloves. "Her hands is awful cold ! Miss Polly, you an' the Captain 'd better pull off'n her shoes an' rub her feet."

"No, I can't do nothin' ! " exclaimed the Captain, weeping like a child.

"Here, let me," said Abercrombie, seeing that everybody was in everybody's way, and the hut had become crowded with confused and helpless people.

Mercy's feet were like stone, so cold and white, and Algie and Aunt Polly, in extraordinary collaboration, chafed them while Mother Margery loosened her clothes and rubbed her hands.

At length, with a shudder, she threw out her

arms and turned her head from side to side, moaning faintly and settled her face against Jack's shoulder without opening her eyes.

The moan was answered by a sigh of relief from those watching about the bed.

Jack's breast thrilled as he drew her imperceptibly closer, and an indescribable look of devotion overspread his ingenuous face.

" Mercy ! " he whispered.

There was no answer, and the watchers waited in silence until she should move again.

The Captain was out on the beach, walking frantically around and around in circles, at intervals rushing up and down the sands and into the cabin as if he were " possessed," gesticulating to himself and sobbing like a child. At last he could bear his anxiety no longer, and, shoving people right and left, he came to the bedside, and, taking Mercy's hand, shook it, saying : " Mercy, can't you wake up no more ? " She shivered, and opening her eyes looked at him in alarm.

" What is it ? " she cried, starting up, staring from one to the other of those whose eyes were fixed upon her. " Oh, I can't think—no —no—I thought it was Jack ! " and she fell back upon his arm again, closing her eyes.

" It is Jack, dear Mercy," he said, " I have come back."

" Dear Jack," said she, opening her eyes and looking at him with a loving smile which gave to her face ineffable beauty. But the effort was too much, and she closed her eyes

again. Her breathing now was less labored ;
and her feet and hands gradually became
warmer. It would have been a boon if she
could have remained quietly sleeping, but
Granny Gooch's bed was not a fit resting place.

" Go, mother, and see how fast the storm
is coming," said Jack ; and having gone to
the door, Mother Margery replied :

" It's a'most here."

" Well, we must get her home at once,"
said he, " and I shall carry her. She mustn't
lie on this bed, and she can't walk."

" No, John, Miss Polly's that contrary, there
ain't no sense goin' agin her."

" She sha'n't stay here, and Miss Polly be
hanged !" said Jack.

" My son, ain't you got no civiler tongue
nor that ?" asked Mother Margery.

" All the same, I mean to carry her. Do
put on her shoes and stockings, and button
up her clothes. I must take her home.
There ain't no time to waste. Git caught
down here in the rain, there won't be no gittin' her home. If you women folks won't put
on her shoes, why let me do it myself. The
ole skipper's that skeered he ain't got no
sense, an' I don't know nothin' 'bout a woman's
clothes."

So Mother Margery, under the influence of
Jack's assertiveness, put the things on, and
Algie buttoned the shoes.

The Captain stood by with the acquiescence
of a man dazed by a blow.

" Now, Captain," said Jack, when all was
ready, " there ain't no use a-wastin' precious
time here talkin'. Mercy wants to sleep ;
she's plumb wore out, and I'm goin' ter take
her straight home to her own bed, if you
ain't got no objections. This ain't the first
time you've seed me tote her, and I'll jest
walk off so." Suiting the action to the word,
without so much as a glance at Aunt Polly,
Jack, who had thews and sinews of iron,
leaned over the bed, picked Mercy up, and
carried her out of the house, whilst she,
opening her eyes, and conscious of her help-
lessness, put her arms around his neck to
steady herself.

" You'll give out afore you git thar !"

"If I do, then you come help," said Jack, in
answer to the voice from the crowd, but whether
in derision or earnest it was hard to tell.

" That's jest the way these peert young 'uns
'll git a-settin' down some fine day," said
Granny Gooch, with bitterness.

" Shut up, you thankless ole hag !" cried a
sailor in reply.

Algie, disgusted at such rudeness, and
sick with emotion, looked about him at the
rough faces which were grave with anxiety,
and gave him little comfort.

He could not bear to follow Jack with
Mercy in his arms. He was so alone amid
all this rude life, glowing with love for her,
that he felt as if he were in a distant land,
where men were speaking among themselves

an unknown tongue. He moved away, assuring himself that the girl's illness was hysteria consequent upon excessive nervous strain, and refusing to believe it heart-disease.

Then, too, Jack had taken her in his arms with such assurance, as if she were his very own, and had shown such affection in every word and glance.

If Abercrombie had been just, he would have realized that a man of such masculinity as Jack's would have acted just so toward any woman who required such help.

Algie must have felt the raw wind cutting him in the face, and heard the thwarted surf raging to reach the cliffs, and seen the clouds sinking lower and lower, and growing blacker even while he walked.

Jack had known their menace, but knew his strength as well ; for many a time he had clung to the sheets when the wind was struggling like a giant in the sail and his arm had seemed as dead. That practiced strength would not fail Mercy in her need.

He might have carried her to his mother's, but it was only a matter of endurance to take her a little farther to the luxury of her own bed.

There was not even a cart-road from the village direct to Blessington House. In summer, or when the day was fair, the men fetched provisions in the boats, which were now rocking distractedly, their keels aground in the shallow water.

12

So now that Jack's strength was essential, he felt an exultation in it joined to a tender sense of possession, as he strode rapidly along, carrying her upon his breast.

When they had gone a third of the way, Mercy whispered to Jack to put her down, and she leaned against him.

" It was my heart," said she. " When I saw you, it gave a great jump and stopped, and my throat got rigid, so that I couldn't move my tongue, and it choked me ; and then everything got smoky, and I didn't know anything more."

Aunt Polly and the Captain overtook them, and presently Mother Margery came up, with Bill Junk and Splugen. The Captain was speechless with delight ; but Mercy, seeing the wet furrows in his cheeks, realized the anguish he had suffered.

"I'm all right now," she said lovingly, "and can walk if I lean against you."

" Let me carry you where the path is narrow," said Jack.

Mercy took her father's arm, and Jack, falling back to join his mother, held her hand quite boyishly as they walked along.

When Abercrombie emerged from the sand-hills, Jack enquired who he was.

" He's a painter man what's come down from Richmond, and is a-stayin' at the Captain's to paint Mercy's picture," replied his mother.

Jack frowned a little, and surveyed Algie with a momentary feeling of suspicion.

But Algie came eagerly forward to congratulate Mercy, and offered her his additional support.

"Thank you, very much," said she, "I'm doing very well, but, as you know already, I have much more confidence in Jack than in myself; and this is Jack!" she exclaimed, turning to present the two men.

"I certainly am glad to see him," said Algie, adding, as he shook hands with Jack, "you never can know how welcome you are back, unless you could know how great was the despair of seeing you again."

Jack looked at Mercy, but, suddenly feeling his heart too full, left them abruptly by the path by which Abercrombie had come.

"Come, mother," he called, "I reckon Mercy don't need us any more now, and home's the place for you.

"Good-bye," he added, nodding once or twice to those he was leaving.

Pulling his soft hat over his eyes, he walked away among the sand-hills, leaving his mother to follow more slowly.

Mercy stood watching them for a second, and then, as if apostrophizing them both, exclaimed. "How good they are, dear souls!"

"Come on, Mercy! don't stand about so long," said Aunt Polly, who, after making every allowance for sentiment, could not feel otherwise than exasperated at Jack's reappearance.

Mercy walked along slowly with her father;

and Abercrombie, silently cursing his luck, was forced to escort Aunt Polly, who bored him intolerably, even to the creaking of her shoes and the crinkling of her stiff silk gown.

When they had reached the house, Mercy wanted to go at once to her room, but the Captain was still in such anxiety that he insisted that Aunt Polly should have a lounge brought into a corner of the dining-room, and that Mercy should be put to bed there, so that he might watch over her without interfering with his daily routine, for there was nothing quite so odious to him as having his regular ways interfered with. He had felt all topsy-turvy for the last three days, and wanted to get head up again without delay.

" I declare, father," Mercy remonstrated, " you must think my wings are ready to fly ! I'm all right, only I'm tired and want rest."

The Captain looked at her with misgiving, while Aunt Polly, with grim impatience, held the door open.

At length the old man followed the girl up the stairs, holding her arm to support her ; while Abercrombie, listening below, heard the murmuring of voices, and Mercy's plaintive protest : " If you will only let me alone—only let me rest."

" For the Lord's sake, Polly, don't be a contraryin' the chile with no more o' your damned talk ! " the Captain had finally exclaimed.

Algie's heart sank within him at the pros-

pect of another day without Mercy. It never
occurred to him to ask himself how he had
endured twenty-six years. He went into the
studio and looked at his picture. The sky he
had thought so fine yesterday looked ghastly
to-day, and he was disposed to fling a brush
at it. How could a man paint when in such
a vile temper! He was about going to his
room when he was amazed to find the Captain
planted like a sentinel beside Mercy's door,
apparently settled there for the remainder of
the afternoon.

"It do pester me so," he began, "to see
folks what won't let nobody alone!"

"Don't be troubled," said Algie, sympathetically, "I think she's all right. She goes
on her nerves until she's nearly dead, but all
she needs to set her up again is rest."

"I'll see to that!" exclaimed the Captain,
shaking his head.

Abercrombie, locked in against intrusion,
sat down in the chair before the fire and determined to be miserable. But he wished to
enjoy that frame of mind in the most thoroughly comfortable way; so he took off his shoes
and put on his slippers, stirred the fire a little,
thrust out his legs until his feet rested on the
fender, and then became luxuriously wretched.
He understood this form of reverie thoroughly, although occasionally his thoughts diverged
from it, just as irrelevant ideas are said to
strike men who are going to be hung. He
leaned the finger-tips of one hand against

the finger-tips of the other, and gazed admiringly at them.

Then he abused his luck and the coast of North Carolina, and wished that that forlorn State had never been discovered, and altogether abandoned himself to feeling as hateful as possible. After a while, a purpose formed amid the chaos of his mind. He must find out the real claims of this Jack O'Doon, since he had so inconveniently come to life again ; or else, he reluctantly added, he must come to some clear understanding of what he himself was about, and not allow this complication to drive him mad. His heart and mind were like two Babes in the Wood—at one moment ready to lie down and die, at another, feeding on crumbs of comfort not bigger than berries.

He thought of Mercy as she lay, silent and white, upon Granny Gooch's bed, and such a pang of remorse smote him that for a moment he closed his eyes, and, as he folded his arms over his breast, his face quivered with the longing he felt for her.

It was the first time his heart had been riven with such yearning for any woman. He knew her now in the extremity of her weakness : before, she had seemed so resolute to help herself, so strong to help others, that he could not realize the spiritual effort which had forced the body beyond its powers. But now, when the body had failed, and the spirit was cowed by a menace from indignant nature, his mind put the query, "What if Mercy really had trouble of the heart, and some fair day, when the flowers were blooming, and the sea-waves shimmering, she should fall again, and there should be no more Mercy?" He could not think of death coming to her, who made gladness for so many, without roses and forget-me-nots.

An awful dread stole over him, and he paced his chamber to and fro. He had shut himself in to coquet with jealousy, and a possibility had struck him as even jealousy could not.

CHAPTER XIV.

HEN Jack and his mother had left
Mercy they passed through the sand-
hills in silence.

Mother Margery's eyes were wept
out and vacant ; and Jack, although so lately
rescued from a cruel death, hung his head with
a blackened brow.   Occasionally his eyes
wandered across the sludges where the water
seeped and oozed among the coarse grasses
as the tide rose.

Both mother and son felt that there was
little to cheer them.

Jack was more wretched than his mother,
because he was more conscious of his misery.

Occasionally a few tears of compassionate
regret came to Mother Margery's eyes, when
she remembered that "Old Ned" had not
been spared to see Jack again. She shrank
visibly from re-entering the cabin whence her
faithful spouse had been carried away forever,
but Jack, when he had opened the door, led
her in.   After placing a chair for her in the
chimney-corner, he brought a great armful of
wood and piled it upon the coals.

The day after a funeral is a grim time and

seems interminable. We get so inured to ghastly thoughts that every pleasant thing in life seems a mockery.

When a man suffers acutely, he endures until he reaches a point whence nature rebounds and declares that any more of that sort of thing is intolerable. Jack just then stood in that regard to death. The loss of his father had been a dreadful blow to him, but he had lately faced such horrors that death at home in a bed was not horrible.

His mother had forgotten him, so he took his sharp knife from his belt and amused himself with splitting up a pine stick to make the fire blaze, for the room was very dark. The narrow window, like a band of light across the eastern wall, revealed nothing save the scurrying clouds without. The tide had turned, and the roar of the waves increased. The wind howled dismally, and the sand scattered down the chimney.

When he looked about the room, he knew he had not been expected. There were no new books, such as Mercy habitually left ; her forethought and care having made it easy, through well-considered marginal notes, for him to get the best out of them. She had devised that means to help Jack educate himself, and make him intimate with her thoughts.

Jack was unreasonable in feeling neglected, for her very anxiety about him had rendered it impossible for her to settle herself to any

work requiring mental effort ; but the recol-
lection of the stranger made him uneasy.

Having been saved from the sea, he had
come home, eagerly anticipating a joyous
welcome. Instead, he had stood unnoticed
beside a fast-filling grave, wonderstruck at
the Captain's words. He had been like an
apparition among those whom he loved, and
even Mercy had been stricken at sight of him.
And, to crown all, this stranger had come,
as Jack mistrusted, to loosen the tie between
her and himself. All other sorrows were
dwarfed by this enormity. It was as the
parting of soul from sense.

What would the devotion of his life count
for against the fascinations of this man of
the world ? He answered himself bitterly :
" Nothing."

The Captain had been poor and earned his
own bread, but had lived to marry a lady.
Why should not he ?

Hitherto, Jack had accepted the difference
between Mercy and himself as the difference
between soul and body ; now, the soul seemed
breaking from its bonds of clay, and the body
was no more necessary to it, but must fall
again to the dust from which it came. Alas !
though his love were as boundless as the ocean
and as fresh as the sweeping breeze, it could
only serve to bear the butterfly floating away
to the sky.

He had never been jealous before. Now
he was almost mad.

"Mother," said he, "I will go and see how the storm holds;" and he thrust his bright knife into its sheath.

Mother Margery arose, and with difficulty they shut the door after him, and she put up the bar within. Jack, at last alone with an immeasurable despair, strode out toward the breakers. The surf was almost upon the sand-cliff, and with a feeling of sympathy he watched the abortive efforts of the mighty waves as they struggled to lick up the bubbles which the shrieking wind had whirled into the seams along the shore.

He looked at the hut, and thought of Mercy in the luxury of her father's house, and laughed contemptuously at himself, and half-pitied his own heart-ache and presumption. He knew, better than any one else, how impossible it was that his longing could ever be fulfilled; but all the same it was there in his breast; and he leaned against the crumbling cliff as if its sands might help him to hold up his heavy heart. He did not heed the wind which was blowing bleak and cold upon his open throat, where the loose collar of his sailor-shirt was turned back from his hairy breast. He was longing to get out upon the sea again. He felt as if he had proven himself invulnerable to death; but the touch of Mercy in his arms had made him faint in his innermost senses, down to his trembling knees.

He felt himself a man, every inch, when he

was straining a mainsheet over a belaying-pin, but here he was no better than a fool ; and from that sickening sense of feebleness he longed to escape—to get away—any-where—even to put half the earth between himself and this fine gentleman ; for Jack was too honest to belittle Abercrombie.

In this state of lonely misery and desire for sympathy, he stood for a long time, mutely looking out upon the sea.

" Perhaps it's for the best," he muttered, as he turned away, " for, after all, I'd give any-thing I possessed to make her happy, and if that's so, I'd better let her alone to be happy after her own heart."

Recalling his mother, he returned to the cabin and rattled the latch. In a moment Mother Margery opened the door for him, and they barred it again behind him. She, too, had come to herself, and when he sat down, put her hands affectionately upon his shoulder, saying :

" You ain't had no fittin' welcome, Jack, but it 'pears like my senses is gone daft this last week." Her tone was apologetic.

" Dear mother," he cried, springing to his feet and embracing her, "don't think of me !" He took her in his arms, and fondly kissed the tear-withered eyelids and the sunken lines which sorrow had made in her cheeks.

" You ain't never told me how you got back," said she, sitting down again, " but I'm jes' that helpless, seems like I ain't got the courage to listen."

" We won't talk about it at all," said Jack, " for it wa'n't so bad but it might ha' been worse, so just don't pester yerself." When Jack talked with his mother or the sailor folk, he lapsed easily into their parlance ; but when he spoke with Mercy, his respect for her, and the influence of her example, made him endeavor to respond to her in good English.

Seeing that his mother was listening, he continued : " I've heard the newspaper stories about never seein' us again, and they were likely enough, for after we'd cut away the ropin' and yards, and flung off the topmast to right ship, though it didn't help her, and sent the masts after 'em, she kept on gettin' worse, seein' as we had such a slippery cargo aboard. We'd pretty much given up all hope, till just as night was comin' on, we struck a current, and drifted ; the Lord knows where we were driftin' to. The waves were rollin' like cliffs and tumblin' down on the deck, and the cold was awful ! The fo'c'sle got beat in, and the bulkheads filled with water, and there didn't seem a livin' chance !

" Jim Simmons got licked off'n the poop, right before our eyes, and none of us ever saw him again.

" Oh, ye ain't got a notion o' what it was like ; and I ain't able to tell you.

" And then we set to workin' the pumps, and we worked till we were worn out ; and it seemed as if our hands would freeze to the pump-handles, it was that cold!

"And the fires got put clean out! Just soaked. The stoves full o' water! So we didn't have any place to warm, and we dasn't walk a step to keep from freezin', for the deck was covered with ice, and as slippery as glass, and slopin' like a house-roof. There wasn't a thing standin' up straight, 'ceptin' o' them things as ought to been crank-sided!

"The wind was drivin' the sleet in our faces, till they were bleedin' awful. I 'most hate to talk about it."

Jack looked into the fire and remained silent.

"Go on," said Mother Margery, who, by a singular process of emotion, found the stirring recital of such active dangers a relief from her memories of the numb apathy in which her husband had died.

"Well," resumed Jack "toward morning, the wind sort o' veered off and the stars came out, a few at a time. The sun rose clear, and the sea was the most beautiful sight I ever saw! Somehow, whenever I'd thought about shipwrecks, I pictured the ships gettin' crushed down into the sea in the dark, and the waves splittin' over 'em like those outside. May the Lord help any poor dog on the sea this night!" said Jack, suddenly pausing to listen, and shuddering as a blast of sand came rattling down the chimney.

After awhile he continued: "But the sun

was that bright it was blindin', and the water
was foamin' and shinin' like quicksilver, and
beatin' over us, glad and mad both.

"There was hardly a chance to get a
mouthful to eat, albeit there was plenty
aboard. Biscuits and junk, and the hold
nigh to bustin' with fish !

"But we dasn't open the main-hatch, for
one of them big waves would have foundered
us alive ; and so we just made a shift o'
eatin' biscuits, a carryin' 'em round in our
pockets.

"Well, we had better weather, and drifted
south-southeast all the next day, as near as
we could tell, for the compass was stove in,
and we pitched about so we couldn't calculate
much by the sun, but nigh on to eight bells
the sea went down, and we set to work to
straighten her out a bit, seein' as we might
keep on floatin' till we came across some sort
o' craft. It got warmer, too, as the wind
slacked, and we emptied the stoves and
managed to get a fire a-goin'.

"But we'd lost our tiller, we didn't have
any canvas, nothin' in God's world to rig her
with, and when night came on, and it got
gloomy and lonesome, Joe Hawkins started
to talk about jumpin' overboard, to keep from
dyin' some worse way. But we all reasoned
with him, and the skipper 'lowed to tie him,
and I reckon maybe now he's glad he held
on.

"We were just like a floatin' island, slap-

pin' around with the wind blowin' us somewhere, though the Lord only knowed where !
But she's a tough old hull, and I'll stand by
her, if ever she puts to sea again ! "

His mother shook her head.

"But one day, seems like it was Friday,
we hove in sight o' one o' them ocean
steamers runnin' between Savannah and New
York.

"Our old skipper hoisted our signal, and it
appeared at first that they didn't want to
notice us, but after awhile they run closer,
and when they came up and took us aboard
were for scuttlin' our old bark, but the
Captain and me, I bein' mate, recommended
to tow her in, for she had an uncommon
tough hull, that brig o' our'n," said Jack,
dropping his voice affectionately, "for if she
hadn't had, I wouldn't be here, that's sure !

"We got into New York yesterday, and
here I be to-day !

"There were lots o' passengers, and the
ladies made a great fuss over us.   One of 'em,
a pretty young one, gave me this.   Took it
out of a hand-bag, and gave it to me."

Jack drew from his pocket a silver flask.

"I reckon she was sorry for me," he said,
as he handed the pretty trifle to his mother.

"I wouldn't mind much havin' a good hot
grog, right now," he added.

"Ye ain't had no dinner, is ye ?" Mother
Margery inquired.

"No, nor breakfast neither, nor supper last

night!" Jack replied, with a sigh at remembering his impatience. "I ain't thought about eatin'. I was so took up with thinkin' about gettin' home. Don't ye disturb yerself. I ain't a sailor if I can't cook."

So saying he filled the iron pot with water, hung it on the crane, and swung it over the fire.

"There's victuals like ez not in the cupboard, my son," said Mother Margery, pointing to the corner.

It was too dark to see distinctly, and Jack picked up a fire-brand to light his movements.

"Will ye eat a ship's pie, mother, if I make it?" he inquired, collecting the ingredients.

"I ain't got no heart to eat, John," she replied; "'pears like this ole cabin ain't nothin' but a big coffin, and I must git away!"

Jack glanced around the quaint place. "'Tain't long since I thought that same thing, mother; but it kind o' hurts me when I hear you say it. Like as not, we won't either of us spend as happy days anywhere else as we've seen and done with, here."

Before Mother Margery could answer, some one rattled the latch, and Jack opened the door to admit a dishevelled child.

"Lord ha' mercy, chile!" cried Mother Margery, bringing the new-comer to the fire, "an' what be you here fur?"

"Mammy sent me ter ax' Jack whar were Grand-daddy Pete. She 'lowed to ha' come her own self, but the baby's that bad she couldn't

13

fetch it, en' I ain't big enough to stay at home
'long o' it."

"And so she sent you over the beach, when
the tide's in, and the quicksands are rottener
than common !" exclaimed Jack.

"I ain't afeared o' nothin' !" replied the
child with assurance, brushing aside the lank
strings of wet hair which fell over her face.

"Your old drunken grand-daddy ain't worth
such a risk !" answered Jack, disgusted.
"Sit down and wait a bit, and I'll go back
with ye a piece as soon as the kettle boils.
Just tell your ma he's safer than he ought to
be, for he ain't any account. Your grand-
daddy was along with us when we were taken
up by a fine big ship, a steamship, chock-full
o' passengers, and they made no end o' fuss
over us. The Captain treated us fine ! He
asked our old skipper and me, seein' as I was
mate, to eat at the Captain's table, and they
gave us no end o' good eatin'. Your old
grand-daddy was in the bulkhead, and the
very first thing he did was to get drunk. I
wish yer ma would let old Pete slide. It's a
shame for her to waste money on him, that
ought to be spent on you little ones.

"All the folks aboard made up a purse for
our men. The skipper and me declined, but
the strange Captain said a speech and gave it
equal around to the others ; and the very first
thing old Pete did, when he got to New York,
was to fetch up at a dram-shop, and spread
himself abeam, dead drunk.

" There he's stranded, and like to stay, as long as he's got a nickel, and I ain't certain when yer ma'll see him ; not before he's starved out, I reckon."

The child grinned as if it were a normal and satisfactory report.

" 'Tain't anything to laugh at, child ! " said Jack, " there ain't any belayin'-pin for ole Pete like a silver dollar before a dram-shop door ! "

" All the folkses down to Hope Shingle axes ye to come down, en' yarn 'em awhile," said the little girl after a pause, looking at Jack with unutterable admiration.

The young sailor was open to flattery, even from a dirty child.

" Tell 'em, when you get home, that I'll try and go to-morrow. I haven't had anything to eat to-day ; I've been in such a mighty on-rest."

The child, at this information, looked hungrily at the beef and pork Jack was mincing on the table, and wonderingly at Jack.

" You must be pretty nigh starved, child," said he, looking at the little girl thoughtfully, " Just keep on sittin' there, and I'll pretty soon give ye a taste o' boilin'-hot ship-pie with inguns in it ! I reckon ye likes that sort, don't ye, honey ? " He said this while scraping together the minced meat and cutting an onion into it, after he had set the spider on the fire, to get hot.

" You didn't know I could cook, did ye ? "

he asked, endeavoring to beguile the time for her. "Ye ain't got an idea o' half what I can do ! Jest you watch me now. Make a good fat short-cake, just so ; put it in the spider ; an' when it's done cookin', just split it open, and fill it cram' full o' hash, and then put it back in the spider, and brown it nice with gravy. Will you tell me I can't cook ? "

The child watched the operation with an interest more vital than curiosity, and promptly accepted an invitation to sit down with him at a table, upon which he had spread a white cloth, and soon afterwards placed two heaping plates of hot pie.

Mother Margery declined to participate, and so Jack made her a cup of tea, and then mixed a mugful of hot grog for himself.

"Did you ever hear o' folk's eyes bein' bigger than their stomicks ? Well that's what they say when little gals like you look as if they wanted to eat all they sees on the table, and their stomicks ain't big enough to hold half. So here's luck to ye ! " said Jack, drinking his grog, "but if ye eat so fast, ye'll choke."

The child devoured her pie in hot haste, pausing at intervals to bestow a look of wondering admiration upon Jack.

"This ain't a real proper sea-pie," said he after a while, with his mouth full—but the child took no exception to that breach of good manners ; "because, in a proper sea-pie, you must keep on pilin' up short cakes, and differ-

ent sorts o' meat, till ye get three or four
decks of 'em ; but this little single-decker, I
reckon, is big enough for you and me. Look
at this here, ain't it a pretty ? "—producing, as
he spoke, the silver flask from his pocket. " A
fine young lady give me that, on the big steamship. I guess you ain't never seen anything
like that before."

The child handled it gingerly with a mute
smile upon her face, but after a moment's re-
flection she asked : " Were she finer than our
Mercy ? "

" No, honey, there ain't anybody finer than
our Mercy," replied Jack, looking caressingly
upon the child, who had unwillingly uttered
the thought nearest his own heart.

"Come, warm up yer toes now, quick as
ever ye can," said he, sitting down on a chair
before the fire, and taking her on his knee ;
" case if ye ain't a-gettin' home pretty quick,
it'll be night, and yer mother'll be that skeered
about you, she'll cry, that she will ! "

Mother Margery was surprised to see Jack's
interest in the little girl, although it never had
surprised her when, since he was a little boy
of seven, and Mercy a baby of one year, he
had devoted himself with indefatigable interest
and ingenuity to pleasing her. " Well, come
on now," said he to the child ; " we'll try it
over the sands. Your little toes ain't snug as
they might be, so I guess I'll tote you some o'
the way."

They opened and closed the door again,

Jack holding it from without while his mother
barred it within, and then he took up the little
maid in his arms, and strode away with her,
moving in the direction opposite to the village.

The surf was heavy and bold, and reached
far into the land ; indeed, in one place, Jack had
to be alert to escape a breaker ; but he carried
the child safely to within sight of her home,
where the beach was wide and sound.

" Now, get along with you," said he, good-
humoredly, standing her on her feet, and
watching her safely started ere he turned to
retrace his steps, looking back from time to
time to see if she were getting on all right.

Jack was devoted to children, and they clung
to him.

Before he returned to his mother's cabin
he took the path to Blessington House, and at
the mess-room door stopped and looked in.
" How's Mercy got ? " said he, refusing the
chair which Bill Junk offered him.

" She's freshin' up a reef," replied Bill, laying down his pipe and urging Jack to sit down
and tell the news.

" What's she doin' ? " inquired Jack, ignoring the other's curiosity, and anxious, yet
afraid, to hear the reply.

" She's a settin' by the fire in the Capting's
ole room, what she an' the young man's a-fixed
up fur a paintin' room—stoody, I b'lieve they
calls it."

Jack's heart sank, but he ventured one more
query. " Is she by herself ? "

" No, indeed, man ; she's a-talkin' to the young gentleman," said Bill.

" But ef she know'd you was here she'd be a-axin' you to come up, Jack," said Splugen, who was Jack's staunch ally.

" Well, I ain't got a mind to interrupt 'em," said Jack sadly ; " but, Tony, I'd be mor'n obleeged to ye ef ye'd fetch me some sort o' book to read," he added, apologetically.

" Here, take this here," said Bill, handing him the last " Century," " take it along. We's done with it ! "

" Give my love to Mercy," said Jack, turning rather dejectedly towards the door. " Tell her I just came by to see ef she were mendin', an' good-bye to ye all. I'll step in again to-morrow, mor'n like."

" There's a storm a-brewin', sure," said Bill, when the door was closed.

" There ain't no better fellow than Jack deservin' to skip a brig," said Splugen, watching him from the window as he passed out of the old oak gate.

Poor Jack, he would have done better to have spared himself that thrust ! But whom had he ever sought with the trust he felt in Mercy ? When had he come home before, and not gone, as soon as he had seen his mother, to spend an hour with her in the friendliest confidence ?

This afternoon he could not face the other man, and his heart was heavy as he turned away ; shrinking from the contrast between himself and Abercrombie, who was so elegant and altogether just what Jack knew that he himself was not.

Jack came and went so noiselessly that Mercy had not heard him as she reclined in her father's chair before the fire, her feet covered with silk stockings and thrust into slippers lined with fur.

She had never before seemed so softly feminine to Abercrombie, her pink gown billowed with lace reflecting a tender glow upon her face.

The Captain was asleep on a lounge beside the chimney, leaving Algie and Mercy to entertain each other.

Presently she roused herself and began talking gleefully. Jack's return had lifted such a weight from her heart.

A golden contrast to Jack himself, who had met nothing but disappointment at every turn, until, looking back at the Jack who had left New York the morning before so full of hope, he could almost have wept for him as for a stranger.

He stood irresolute when he had closed the gate behind him, and pressed his hand to his eyes to blur the tears which he scorned to shed. But he could not repress the heaving of his breast nor the shudder that shook his frame.

Till now he had been content with things as they were, believing that if he did his best something would come to his aid before it was too late.

He suddenly flung out his arms and clasped them behind his neck, and looked up to God inquiringly—then wished he were dead, and a cruel temptation came to him.

Looking at the sea, he pondered, knowing there was a certainty of escape. The night was closing in ; the water was boiling and black ; but a holy and generous thought rescued him in his temptation.

A tender smile overspread his face.

" Perhaps I have been spared to help Mercy," he said to himself. " Who knows how soon the hour may come when she will need some one who loves her to help her, and I will be that one, even though she does not love me now, and cannot love me then."

Jack's great sympathy with the sea enabled him to find relief for his own emotion in its turbulence, and as he gazed upon it his heart found the peace of passive endurance.

Jack's was a chivalrous heart, and his outward roughness did not prove him less noble than many a knight who, in olden times, buckled his lady's sleeve in his helmet and fought for love and died.

In his expanding eyes there was the power of a heathen god's, and when he was angry, men let him alone ; for it was a power of authority, and his eyes glowed until all else was lost to sight, even the lion-like strength of his shoulders.

Thought of one woman only could soften them, and bring a veil over them as now, when he felt that he could not endure the fainting confidence within.

As he neared his mother's cabin, Jack observed that no smoke issued from the hole in the sand-hill. She had let the fire go out, and his conscience smote him that he had forgotten her.

The cabin was utterly black within. Mother Margery sat moping beside the hearth. He could scarcely find her. When he had rekindled the fire, he went to a place in the wall, removed the canvas hanging, and opened a door behind it, disclosing a smaller cabin with a single bunk and locker. On a shelf at the head of the berth stood a good lamp.

" How is it, mother," said he, returning with it to the table, " that you never will use my lamp when I am gone ? "

" I am used to the firelight, John," said she. " When a body works from early mornin' through a long day, they are glad to rest when the sun sets, an' I can rest better in the dark. I ain't no scholar, my son, as ye well knows," she added sadly. Mother Margery's speech, innocent of grammar, had a pathos in it to the ears of poor Jack, which made him careful of assuming anything better to her, lest he should sound fine. At sea, too, his men best understood the vernacular to which they were accustomed, and so Jack kept up the two forms of speech, as if they were two languages ; like work-a-day and holiday clothes, to be put on, or laid by as occasion might require.

When he wrote, his diction was good ; so
that seeing Jack in his mother's hut, speaking
the dialect of the fisher-folk, acknowledging
his birthright among them, we see him at his
worst ; but that worst was none the less
noble because it was a voluntary sacrifice to
the pride of others.

Jack, like all other men, was perforce ot
two natures; although the refined inner one
seldom saw the light.

He despised the thought of setting up to be
finer than the old sailor his father. Only
Mercy knew both natures well, and it was the
secret self which was suffocated to-night for
want of her. But all the same, he sat down
beside the light and looked at the pictures in
his book, although at times his eyes were
blank of sight. He had so much to tell Mercy,
and was so disappointed not to have seen
her.

He missed his father's occasional groan
from the chimney-corner. His mother had
generally been silent—now she was hoarse
with weeping, and the moan from time to
time, with which she changed her position,
wrung his heart. It seemed as if he could not
possibly endure anything more. He closed
the book and looked into the blaze, and listened to the wind shrieking outside, and
watched the sporadic flames pop up between
the logs.

It was not yet eight o'clock. The gloom
was utterly lifeless. He was terribly weary,

but the night was so long, and he disliked leaving his mother to spend it alone.

"Mother, won't you eat something?"

"No, boy, I ain't got no taste for nothin'."

Another gloomy silence, until Jack thought he should go mad.

At last, casting her eyes upon him for a moment, she saw that he was weary, and urged him to go to rest.

With some reluctance he exchanged the fireside for his bed, and fell into a death-like sleep. Thus ended that dreadful day.

CHAPTER XV

F surcease of suffering be happiness, lulled by "Nature's soft nurse," Jack had been happy, and sunshine streamed through a chink in the roof ere he awoke and made ready to take up the burden of another day.

Outside, wreaths of pink clouds half encircled the ascending sun, and the gray silhouette of a ship was passing across the disk. Sunshine gladdens the soul, and Jack, whose heart was ready for beneficent influences, felt a kind of joy in the brightness of the morning, as he wandered, gathering here and there the debris cast ashore by the storm. The water-soaked fragments had a different meaning to him now, and he wondered if any of the splinters he held had fallen from his own hand and been cast from the " Marianetta."

He bestirred himself to relieve his mother of her work ; for even Granny Gooch could not deny that he was a good son.

The April morning was seductively penitent, after the raging night, and mother and son sat down to breakfast with the cabin door open, and the bright light streaming in,—a noble picture against the background of sail-cloth. Their faces contrasted strangely. Jack's was eloquent with strength of purpose, brilliant in coloring, and vivid with the ardor of youth. His eyes, of a deep brown, were set beneath jet-black brows, which met together; and his hair and close-cut beard were tinged with chestnut in the lights, and umber in the shadows.

Mother Margery was stately and silent, and her face, colorless and careworn, was sombre with grief.

The copper kettle hissed audaciously in their faces, its bloated form red and shining. Jack made tea for his mother, their breakfast consisting of fish and brown bread, served on pewter platters. The world did not seem such a bad place as it had appeared the night before.

Most unexpectedly, Mercy appeared at the door. Jack welcomed her eagerly, and poured out a cup of tea for her, while Mother Margery laid a plate upon the table.

"I can only stop for the tea, thank you," said she; "I have stolen away from home, and father must not miss me. But I did so want to see you, Jack."

She spoke frankly, and with such earnest affection that it augured poorly for Jack's hopes of love.

"Splugen told me you were at the house yesterday evening, and I think it was so mean of you not to come upstairs and see me," she said, while Jack, leaning with his elbows on the table, watched her sipping her tea.

"I thought you had better company," he replied, bashfully.

Mercy looked at him with troubled inquiry in her eyes, and then blushed crimson, but recovered herself sufficiently to stammer : "A fair exchange is no robbery."

Mother Margery looked with curious interest from one to the other.

"I came to hear about the shipwreck, Jack," said Mercy, after a long pause. "If Mother Margery has heard it, let's go and sit upon the old keel, and you tell me everything ; I'm not at all hungry."

Jack complied, and she sat watching the shimmering sea while he told her the story he had told his mother.

As he finished, Mercy wiped her eyes, and then both were silent while they watched the distant sails as they passed and vanished like phantoms along the misty line which lies between the ocean and the sky.

After a while Jack said : "But all the time, Mercy, I was thinking of you, and it seemed to me that if I could hold on to life long enough to see your dear face again, I could go better satisfied into the other world and wait until I should find you there. If I had never known you, I could not have endured the suffering it cost to get home ; and perhaps none of us would have been alive this morning ; for there were so few—only nine all told—that if one had

failed, the others could not have held out.
Hour by hour, life did not seem worth the living ; and now that I am with you again, dear
Mercy, I feel as if I never wanted to take my
eyes off your face."

"Jack," said Mercy, earnestly, "you blind
yourself to all but the best in me."

"No, that's not so," said Jack with assurance. "I never talked like this to you before,
because until I felt that all the world was
being taken away, I did not realize the value
I put upon the things in the world. But that
awful night was a 'Last Judgment' to each
of us, and I knew then that whatever you
might feel for me, I loved you more than anything. I know just what big notions your
father and your Aunt Polly have got for you,
but my strength is yours, Mercy ; the strength
of my heart and of my soul, and you have only
to ask for it. You are my bright star, far
away out of reach, but I never mean to look
lower."

Mercy's eyes rested on Jack's face with a
pathetic smile, although tears were very near
her lashes. He was so close and dear ; but
she was too like him to love him.

But Jack held his world in his gaze as his
glowing eyes rested on her face. Mercy,
looking up, encountered their intense passion.

"Do not go home that way," said Jack,
moving after her as she turned from him.
"I'm so afraid of the quicksands ; if a drift is
cast on them one day, the next it is gone. It

seems to me that the vein is getting wider and rottener than it used to be."

"I have a terror of it too," said she. "It would be such a frightful thing to be buried alive that way."

"I can't bear the thought," said he, "it makes my flesh creep! Don't ever go by the North Beach. It terrifies me to think of any danger befalling you, or any other sort of trouble, Mercy. But, if anything should happen, you would come to me, wouldn't you? You know, I know what intensest suffering is, and oh, believe me when I say I would do anything, even die for you!"

He grasped her arms and held her for a moment, looking at her, and his eyes seemed to penetrate the secret of her heart. Mercy could not withstand the fascination of them, as he slowly added:

"I have begun to think I could even give up my life to save the life of another man, if I believed that you loved him, and that such an exchange could make you happy."

Such words might have seemed idle vaunting in another, but in Jack's life he had never promised aught which he had not fulfilled. He waited to see if she understood him, and then released her, and they walked along the path to her father's house. Suddenly he stopped again, and, standing in front of her, blocked the way.

"Will you promise me that you will come to me for help if I can give it? You always

14

have laughed at my superstitions, but lately
a pink curlew was shot and fell at my feet.
That's a rare bird for this time o' year, and
my favorite bird, too, and I can't help asso-
ciating it with you, and thinking you'll need
me."

Mercy laughed at the idea. "It was my
fainting yesterday, depend upon it. You have
already picked up your poor bird out of the
dust and carried her home, so be satisfied,
Jack, that you have done the very best for
me."

Jack shook his head. "I'm going to your
father this morning to ask him for a berth,
and if he has none ready I shall try a foreign
one. Can I do anything for you before I
go?"

Now in time past, had Jack told Mercy that
he was going away indefinitely she would
have clung to his hands, and with tears in her
eyes have implored him to stay, appealing to
him in behalf of his mother. But to-day she
was absent and perplexed. Her conscience
was struggling. She was saying to herself,
was it right to wish to keep him here, when
she knew she could never be his wife, and it
behooved her to send him into the world that
he might meet other women and forget her.

What was the adage she had heard, "A
sailor finds a love in every port"? Mercy
knew little of life, but she fancied it might be
true; and doubtless it was because Jack
knew but this one port that he loved her.

She looked at him—at his sturdy figure, his hard hands—one was marked with a blue anchor—at his muscular throat ; but then she let her glance fall. She dared not look into his burning eyes, and meet that conquering gaze, the look which made men obey him, young or old. But, had she done so, she would have seen instead such tenderness as she had never known existed in the world.

Mercy was cold, but it was the coldness of innocence. Truly, what did she know of love ?

Women need to be educated in love. She had never before been talked to of it. There is a contagion in the magnetism of a man's passion which she had never felt.

Jack did not again speak of himself, and they walked on in silence till they reached the garden gate. Here he took her hand, as they stood behind the screen of the wall, and kissed it reverently.

Truly, Mercy was gaining experience, and her education might fairly be said to be begun. Jack blushed at his own hardihood, and Mercy being equally embarrassed, they parted without a word.

Jack having thus placed himself in a new attitude toward her, she felt that she had lost a friend ; she did not know the value of a lover ; so she did just what every foolish young woman is apt to do, when there is no one to prevent it. She ran up to her own room, shut the door stealthily, and then threw herself down on her bed, and sobbed fit to break her heart, and why ?

Crying for Jack. The old Jack that had passed away. The friend she could not exchange for the lover. And yet there was an inner consciousness in her heart, that Jack had a power strong enough to make himself her master. But no, she did not love Jack, not that love !

Her cheeks were blistered till they burned, and her eyelids so swollen that when she came down to breakfast she looked a fright, and astonished every one by her unaccountable appearance.

CHAPTER XVI.

"ORD A'MIGHTY! Why, Mercy, what ye been doin' to yerse'f?" cried the Captain, putting down his spectacles from the top of his head, and leaning across the corner of the table to look closely into her face.

"I've been to see Jack," she replied.

"Been to see Jack!" he repeated. "Why, I've been a crawlin' aroun' on tiptoe this here two hour! I thought you was abed. Didn't holler, nor nothin'! I ain't got no 'pinion o' that Jack o' your'n. He ain't never so much ez come a-nigh me sence he come home. A prowlin' roun' here las' night too, I hear'n."

"He probably thought you were taking a nap," said Mercy, "and no doubt you were; but he wants to go to sea again, and is coming to find out if there is a berth for him. If there isn't, he intends to ship on a foreign line."

"Them foreign boats be hanged to 'em!" cried the Captain angrily, laying down a spoonful of soft-boiled egg, to vent his intolerance.

"I wish you'd make him captain of the next new boat you get," said Mercy.

"Captain!" roared the skipper in astonishment. "Why, he ain't nothin' but a boy!"

"He's twenty-four years old," said Mercy, "and every man and boy you've got says he's the bravest and best of them all. Good sound sense and courage and honesty are all you want, and who has more, or knows more about a ship than Jack?"

"Look-a-here, did he tell you to make that fine speech to me, young woman?" said the Captain suspiciously, scrutinizing her face.

"Jack tell me! Why no, of course not! I don't suppose he ever thought of such a thing; but all the same, I wish you'd do it."

A long silence ensued. The Captain wrestled with an idea.

Algie, sitting opposite Mercy, had been listening with eager interest to this dialogue. He would have been overjoyed if the Captain had promoted Jack to be admiral of the whole flotilla, or anything in reason which would remove him without injury. This thing of being obliged to witness Mercy fainting at sight of him, then carried off like the Anados, and now, when every one supposed her still sleeping, to see her appear with red eyes and blistered cheeks, and hear her coolly declare she'd been to see Jack, and had evidently been weeping over his adventures, was simply insufferable! He was indignant, and gave his entire attention, apparently, to fresh mackerel and toast.

"Who knows," thought he, "that fellow

Jack may have caught this very fish I am eating."

Aunt Polly looked disdainfully across the tea-things, and ignored the conversation.

So the meal was finished in silence, and afterwards the Captain drew a very long breath, and went forth to take a constitutional up and down the garden path. He was deep in problematical thoughts, whiffing his long reed-stemmed pipe, and blowing smoke out of a corner of his mouth.

Finally he pushed his hat back and wiped his brow with his red handkerchief, as if his thoughts were fatiguing him. Algie lighted a cigarette, and he and Mercy went to work in the studio.

After an hour's chattering and some work, Algie exclaimed, "I think it is a shame for us to lose this magnificent light. Suppose we begin the picture, if you feel able to pose, after you have rested. Meantime I will lay fresh colors, for these are getting stale."

So he brought out his paint-box and sat down beside her, placing the box on his knees, while he scraped off the hardened paint, and reset the palette.

"Do you always keep the colors so?" asked Mercy, pointing to the palette, which was particularly brilliant and harmonious.

"Yes, it is a great beauty to have a hand-some palette; and this appearance can only be acquired with long use. You see the centre and the right hand have acquired this

dim gray, and brilliancy with polishing, while
the blending of the ingrained colors of this
setting is as rich as an India shawl. This one
is my pet. If you really mean to paint, I shall
leave it with you as a precious keepsake ; for I
will never use it again after painting your picture, and I shall want you to have something
I really value, to remind you sometimes of
me."

Abercrombie looked at Mercy, who dropped
her eyes quickly. He was sincere while he
spoke. Who can blame him, if time and tide
wait for no man, and if, ere he was ready, he
were forced to turn with the tide. But let the
tide turn when it might, he was absolutely in
earnest in every word he uttered to Mercy
during his stay at Blessington House. She
glanced coyly at him ; and sincerity, even the
sincerity of a fickle man, has something so
convincing in it, that she believed him, and
replied with equal truth : "Will you really ? I
shall love so to have it. But there is no chance
of my forgetting you, for I am accused of being
one of those dreadful people who never forget."

"Oh, but you must remember me for imaginary virtues, and not for actual faults. Let the
absent be ever justified—or—what is the adage
I am trying to quote ?"

"I could not imagine myself remembering
you, except in the most agreeable and charming way," replied Mercy, quite coquettishly,
unconsciously returning the slight smile with
which Abercrombie was regarding her.

" I do not quite know whether you're laughing at me or not. I'm afraid I have a tutored dread of people who never forget. They are also the people who never forgive, aren't they ? "

" That must depend upon what you mean by forgiving," said Mercy.

" I mean the opposite of spitefulness and unforgivingness," replied Algie.

" As regards myself, I am just as much in the dark as ever," said Mercy. " I would not harm a hair of the head of any one who had harmed me, and I think I could and would be kind to such a one to the day of my death, but I'd remember the injury all the same. I cannot forget that Granny Gooch abuses me whenever I go near her, but that would not delay me for a moment from taking her something to eat again as soon as I could."

" Perhaps that is the charity which covers a multitude of sins," said he.

" Perhaps so," said she indifferently.

" Still," he persisted, " you have not promised me to forgive me in advance if ever I offend you."

" I do not fear any evil from you," said Mercy with a smile. The expression of her face was so soft and confiding that Abercrombie felt his heart rise in his throat, and he turned away from her with a sudden movement.

" But all the same," he added after a pause, " if you ever had cause to think ill of me, would you forgive me ? "

" I would never harm you, but I could not forget it unless I could forget you, not if I lived a million years. You would be a unit to me, but a unit with the blemish of an offence, because a man's actions are essentially a part of himself."

" I had hoped," said Abercrombie, moving aside to arrange his canvas, " that I might in time be something more than a cipher to you, but if, at the end of a million of years, I am to find myself only a unit, I fear I shall be immortal before I become more."

Mercy blushed and looked thoughtfully into the fire. Abercrombie's facile and fluent tongue had uttered a thousand such pretty speeches and poured them into the ears of fair and willing listeners who had pleased him momentarily; and he was always sincere at the time—just as sincere as Jack was, or anybody else,—too sincere, because he was so dazed by the glow of his own imagination that he failed to see the injustice of his impulses, and under the enthusiasm of the moment went rashly along pathways that he was sometimes obliged to retrace with sorrow.

When he had arranged the light to his satisfaction, he was wishing for an old gray sail-cloth to use as a back-ground for Mercy, as that, in the strong light, would have much the same effect as the sky of his picture.

" I will send to Jack for one," said Mercy promptly.

" It seems to me you depend upon Jack for

everything ! " exclaimed Algie, irritably. " He is perfectly ubiquitous—turns up everywhere —from the grave itself ! "

Mercy looked at him in astonishment, and was perplexed at seeing an impatient frown upon his face.

She answered rather tartly, " I suppose the natural reason is that Jack is always to be de pended upon. He is found where he is wanted, always does well what he undertakes to do, and if he does not make life a success for himself, does so for other people. Consequently, if I send to Jack for the sail-cloth, I'm certain it will be exactly what you want," and she suited the action to the word.

A silence ensued between them. Mercy stood on the rug, looking into the fire. Both she and Abercrombie felt contrite, but each hesitated to make an overture. Algie oiled his canvas and afterwards diligently rubbed off the oil.

" Why did you do that ? " asked Mercy.

" Because if the pores of the canvas are moist with oil, the fresh paint I put on to-day will readily combine with what I put on on Monday, and there will be no difference of feeling between them."

" *Feeling ?* " said Mercy interrogatively.

" *Feeling*, in painting," said Algie, " is a reflex term. If I rubbed your finger with sandpaper, it would be you who would feel instead of the paper. One layer of paint lying harshly upon another would irritate your taste in much the same way, and I should say the paint felt harsh or the _feeling_ was wrong. _Comprenez-vous ?_ "

" _Parfaitement_," replied Mercy ; " but you would better not draw me out in French," she added, laughing, " for I think you would die of internal convulsions ; though I know you would be much too kind to laugh outright at me ! "

" Try me," said Algie. " It will give you a happy expression for your picture, beside the charity of relieving me of the hard work of my own thoughts."

After a little persuasion Mercy essayed to speak French with him, and Algie was surprised, not only at the large number of words which she knew, but at the atrociousness of her pronunciation. He was bravely polite ; but they were both at last in convulsions of laughter, when Jack entered the room with a great bundle of sail-cloth over his shoulder.

Mercy and Algie looked so strangely and exasperatingly on free and easy terms to poor Jack, that he stood abashed at his unannounced intrusion, and did not speak a word.

" Come in, Jack, it was so good of you," said Mercy, eagerly going forward to meet him. " I did not mean that you should trouble yourself to bring it to us."

That " _us_ " was an outrage to Jack. When had serving her been a trouble to him. " I was nearly here when I met Splugen," he explained apologetically, " so I walked back to

the village and uncorded the gaff." Sure
enough, the stout fellow had borne the spar
upon his shoulder, with the sail suspended
from it. It was well he had done so, for the
gaff answered all the purposes of a curtain
bar, upon which the sail moved easily with its
rings ; and Jack, with handy readiness, adjusted
it diagonally across the corner of the room.
Thus the mildewed sail gave the " values " of
a mottled sky behind Mercy's figure.

Jack's ready understanding, despite his ignorance of the requirements of a studio, and
the vagueness of the message Splugen had
carried, aroused Algie's admiration, and Mercy
could not resist exchanging a glance with him
which meant, " I told you so."

" Sit down with us, Jack," said Mercy, en-
treatingly. " Come, take my chair by the fire ;
and now that everything is ready, shan't I
stand for you, Mr. Abercrombie, and Jack can
tell you if I am looking my best ? "

Mercy placed herself before the screen, and
Jack, leaning with his elbow upon the mantelpiece, observed the gentle, slight, and deferen-
tial touches with which Abercrombie arranged
her pose.

It was hard for Jack, although it interested
him deeply, despite the torment of it, and he
continued standing, silently watching Algie,
while he laid on the masses.

" I will stop now for a little while," said the
artist at length. " You begin to look pale, and
I cannot, therefore, put in the face. But I'm

glad I have such a happy effect in the mass of the drapery."

"What do you mean by the mass?" said Mercy.

"I think I shall write a book," said Algie, laughing, "and call it ' Experiences with an audience of one.'"

At this remark Jack made a little movement, as if he felt *de trop*.

"Pray do not go," exclaimed Algie, " ' the more the merrier.'" This remark, accompanied by his most cordial smile, appeased Jack's sensitiveness, and he sat down near Mercy on the lounge, which had been drawn up beside the fire.

"Shall the lecture be in French, Miss Blessington?"

"Oh, pray forbear!" cried Mercy, adding, as she turned toward Jack: "Do you know, when you came in, I was trying to talk French! Mr. Abercrombie had endured it like a Spartan for a good half-hour, and had just broken down."

So that was what they were laughing about! Not so bad after all, thought Jack.

"Enough is as good as a feast," continued Mercy, "so let me enjoy the freedom of my native tongue."

"Well, ladies and gentlemen," began Algie, pompously, " you two must imagine I'm before the footlights, with *thousands* of people listening ; those of you who in early youth have indulged the charms of moonlight will readily understand mass without detail. No, but really," said Algie, gravely, " on a moonlight night we see the mass only, because the light is not strong enough to develop the detail. The tone is too black, because the high lights are not high enough, and the shadows are not mitigated by reflected lights. Therein is the charm of moonshine ; it appeals to the imagination, and rests the eyes and brain, after the multiplicity of details and excessive realism of broad daylight."

This explanation was satisfactory to Jack, and he thought he liked Abercrombie. Who could know Algie and not like him ? His manners were so simple, and his voice and smile had the ingenuousness of a child's. It was the most charming art, because it was the completion of nature, not its affectation. He imitated nothing, but he had the wisdom of a man of the world, and the taste of a gentle-man, to show himself to the best possible ad-vantage to every one.

At this moment Aunt Polly, coming down-stairs for a walk, looked in at the door. She nodded distantly to Jack, and retired. Poor Jack, he could not conceive what he had done to provoke Aunt Polly to assume this half-dis-dainful manner toward him.

Algie resumed his palette, and Mercy posed again.

It seemed to Jack that he had never seen her look quite so lovely as she did that morning.

It was very mild weather. The fire died

out, and the sunshine streamed in at the window, so that Algie was obliged to stretch a sheet across it, and when Antonio announced that lunch was ready, he declared that the morning had been altogether too short.

"Come along, Jack," said Mercy; "Mother Margery can spare you, and you shall sit by me."

Jack looked at his hands, which he had forgotten, and which were besmeared with grease from the socket of the gaff.

"I see you are a subject for Bill Junk," she said. "Run down, while we wait for you."

So Jack disappeared below, and soon returned, looking very smart and handsome in his burly, picturesque way; and, much to Algie's surprise, they all sat down to table together.

"By Gimmeny!" cried the Captain, at the sight of Jack, "you're a fellow!"

Mercy smiled, for she knew the import of her father's ejaculations. They were oracular, and "By Gimmeny" was of good omen. Then she recalled his preoccupied walk in the garden, and "By Gimmeny" meant that it had begotten something satisfactory, of which Jack was the subject. Her spirits went up accordingly.

"I heerd ye run afoul o' a storm," said the Captain, sitting down and putting his elbows on the table, and looking at Jack inquiringly out of his shrewd gray eyes.

"The sea were pretty roughish," said Jack,

relapsing at once into grammar which rivalled the Captain's own.

"Yes," drawled the Captain, "I've had a visitor what give me a longer account o' it than that, young man."

All eyes were turned in astonishment toward the Captain. . "You young uns," he continued viciously, "is bin keepin' up such a cacklin' and jabberin' in thar, it's no sort o' wonder ye can't hear nothin' but yerselves. Mercy, he sent his love to you."

Both of the young men looked up, and Abercrombie asked himself, "Whose turn next?" He even looked upon his own susceptibilities as less meretricious since he at least had grace enough to have done with one affair before embroiling himself in another. But here was Mercy, with a third man sending his love to her.

"Sent his love to me!" exclaimed Mercy, incredulously. "Why, who in the world was it?"

"Do you suppose it were any young idjut? I've got enuff o' them sort, closer home," casting a baleful glance around the table. "Why, Freemantle, of course! Who else were it like to be, reportin' to me, arter gettin' wrecked on one o' my boats. Which is sayin' more for his manners than some other folks I knows on!"

"I was on my way to speak to you when I met Splugen, but Mercy——"

"Jest you stop right thar," interrupted the

15

Captain. "I'm gittin' tired o' havin' Mercy flung at my head all day long, an' all night too for that matter; fur it's a-gittin' that awful, I jes' dream about it nights!"

The Captain had a good appetite, notwithstanding this atrocious filial nightmare.

"I declar' before the Lord," he ejaculated with a sigh, when he had finished his soup, "an' you young uns will find out soon enough from experience, that a man ain't o' no use in God's world, but to be trampled on by the women folks in his family! I pities men, they's so down-trod! See me! One might have expected to find a clattering skeleton. Here I've lived in this world fifty-seven years, to be nuthin' at last but a figur'-head, a darned ugly one at that, but all the same, to be a figur'-head, to run my ole nose into every sea what comes, that this here young woman might ride on my back and steer me 'roun' to suit her own notions!" The Captain dammed his farther utterance by cramming his mouth full of bread, but he went on mumbling while he chewed it, until after a while the words could be distinguished—"I suppose you ain't got no more use for the sea, is ye, Jack?"

"Yes, Captain, I was comin' up this mornin' to ax ye if ye had a berth open for me; seein' ez how the ole hull ain't like to be set to rights afore next season."

"Well, I ain't concluded nuthin' yet, young man," drawled the Captain, looking at Jack

out of the corner of his eye, "but ole Freemantle do say it warn't right to let ye slide ;
an' nobody shall say o' Solomon Blessin'ton,"
he continued, in his most spread-eagle manner,
leaning back in his chair, and thrusting his
thumbs into his arm-holes, "nobody shall
say that Solomon Blessin'ton ain't got no appreciation o' the genuine thing ; and what's
more, nobody shall say ez what Josiah Freemantle do say ain't the *Lord's truth !*"

He uttered these last words very emphatic-
ally, and, leaning forward, looked at Jack as if
he were going to eat him. Mercy and Abercrombie looked on in breathless expectation.

"And what do you 'uns all think Freemantle do say?" The Captain glanced inquiringly around, scowling at each one in
turn ; then his countenance relaxed and he
continued : "Why, Lord-a-massy, to begin
with, he were that upset he drunk a pint o'
grog, hot at that, afore he found his tongue,
an' he did say that 'ef it hadn't a bin fur that
boy'—he was a meanin' you, Jack—'ef it hadn't
a bin fur that boy, we wouldn't none o' us a
got home.'"

"There ain't no tellin' what a man won't
say when he's dun drunk a pint o' grog," said
Jack, completely overcome with confusion, and
blushing painfully.

"Lord, ef he ain't ez red ez a gal !" cried
the Captain, enjoying the whole thing immensely. Mercy put her hand under the table-
cloth, and patted Jack's hand affectionately.

"Well, Freemantle says, says he, 'that boy'—meanin' o' you, Jack—' is got more sense nor ten men, and he's got,' says he, ' hands afore an' hands behind o' him, an' legs the same, and wits to match 'em all.'"

The Captain paused long enough for Abercrombie and Mercy fully to conceive this monster, and then proceeded. "'That's a queer sort o' a boy,' says I to him. Did ye ever hear o' sech a kind o' a thing down in your parts, Mr. Applecorn?"

Algie denied promptly.

Jack was ready to melt with fervent heat, and Mercy again caressed his hand under the table-cloth.

"An' bein' ez Freemantle says he ain't got no wife, an' no childern, an' he's got about his stomachful o' salt water arter this here dose, he's a mine ter give up the ship, an' what does ye think o' that fur a ole fool?" demanded the Captain, suddenly pausing, and scowling at Jack, but Mercy discovered a twinkle in her father's eye.

"And so," she interrupted, eagerly clapping her hands, " you are going to buy a new brig and give it to Jack! Oh, Jack, you lucky old boy!" she exclaimed, jumping up from the table and rushing toward him. She looked as if she were going to embrace him, but recovered her senses, and hugged her father instead.

"I ain't never said the word," cried the Captain, pretending to suffocate, but beaming with delight. " Look here, gal. I'd like to know somethin' about this here business. Whose a-gettin' this here ship, what's a gwine to break me right now to buy ? You er Jack ? Fur it do 'pear to me like ye was a-tryin' to boss the whole business ! "

The Captain, in the presence of the new idea, turned upon Jack his inquiring eyes ; but Jack was leaning with his chin upon his palm, and was watching Mercy and the Captain with speechless emotion, and a young hero's tears of passionate gratitude at this recognition of his courage were glittering in his eyes.

" Dear Jack," cried Mercy, looking at him a moment inquiringly, and then, overcome by her sympathy and joy for him, she lifted his face with her hands, and wiped the tears from his eyes with her handkerchief, kissing him tenderly, while Jack, with unutterable devotion, clasped his arms for a moment around her waist.

" You will never regret it, father," said she with certainty, resting her hands, while she spoke, upon Jack's shoulders, and displaying the pride and assurance of one who guarantees her own as equal to any possible demand ; and tears trembled and fell from her lashes and splashed upon Jack's hair.

Algie, whose ready sympathies were with the young man, turned his eyes away to relieve his embarrassment, feeling that the scene was too sacred for his scrutiny. In doing so he encountered the stony look of indignation with which Aunt Polly was regarding Mercy. It was sufficient to inspire Algie with the most sudden and implacable aversion for her. It had never occurred to him to misconstrue Mercy's impulsive demonstration toward Jack ; on the contrary, it had shown to him that she must feel for Jack only as toward a brother ; and it inspired him with a tender reverence for her guileless simplicity. He argued very justly to his own mind, that it was because the kindness Jack had found so overwhelming had been of Mercy's own seeking that she wished to share his blushes and embarrassment.

The Captain was greatly moved by Jack's modesty, and blew his nose violently, and winked persistently at Sailor, who endeavored to elucidate the complication by climbing upon his master's knee.

"I declar' I never see the like ! " cried the ·Captain impatiently. "Such a fellow, two such of 'em ! " he added, dimly forgetful of Mercy's sex. "I do declar' before judgment, that ef Freemantle wasn't a man what never praised nobody, I'd give up, ef I thought such a red-faced, blushin' boy were fit to have no ship at all ! But Freemantle do say, and he ain't no liar, that that very boy," shaking his finger at Jack, "were the very backbone o' the whole crew. An' look at him ! "—they all looked at him out of the corners of their eyes. " Fetch her out, Tony, an' boost him up ! "

But Tony was not anywhere to be seen. He had slipped out silently, and his dry old bones had long ago rattled down the stairs to carry the news to the "watch below."

After luncheon was finished there was nothing for Mercy to do but go home with Jack to tell Mother Margery the news, laughing, and dangling upon Jack's arm as they hurried along, and Algie was left to sulk.

CHAPTER XVII

HE happy April days were gone, the picture was finished, and Abercrombie had no longer excuse to linger.

He had not yet uttered to Mercy the words "I love you," but every smile and glance had told her so. When his conscience took him to task, in the dark hours of the night, he had protested it was honor which held his tongue. He must pay his debts and get ahead. He could not marry her for her father's money; and so he went about breaking her heart instead.

One thing unsettled his resolution.

He, too, had begun to rely upon Mercy to direct his conscience, but upon this momentous subject he could not consult her. He could not put the query, "Is it right for a poor fellow like myself to offer you his heart and hand, when the hand is full of unpaid bills, and the heart, by force of habit, is disreputably uncertain?"

The true difficulty was that though he loved Mercy much, he loved Algernon Abercrombie more. If he were rich, he was kindly certain,

he would marry her on the spot ; but he could
not brook the thought of humiliating himself
to ask for Mercy's money along with herself.

He shrank with secret dread from leaving
her ; and she, scarcely knowing her own mind,
exerted herself to keep him. Hitherto every
wish of her heart had been gratified—even Jack,
who had been as dead, had returned living ;
but this wish, so vital and so dear, only Abercrombie could gratify, and he put his vanity
as a fetish before him, and bowed down and
worshipped it, calling it his integrity, and
sacrificing Mercy to the false god.

During the last days Abercrombie had
spent every waking hour at her side ; and he
was so brilliant and so clever that she depended
upon him as upon an inspiration, and did not
miss Jack, who was forever running off to
Richmond to see after the new ship which was
being fitted out under his supervision.

Mercy had an advantage in knowing nothing
of Abercrombie's previous flirtations, since
the knowledge would have made her less confiding. It was her trust in him, beyond all
else, which endeared her to him. The thought
that she would suffer if he neglected her, made
him miserable.

He told her he would return to Cassandra
Bay before the summer was gone, and they
planned excursions together on the map.

It was the last evening, and they sat near
the easel upon which stood the little picture
he had first painted.

" You can never know how I shall treasure this," said he, resting his hand lovingly upon the sketch, and looking at her as if he wished that he could drink the heart out of her eyes ere he left her. Her eyes lingered timidly, bewilderedly, answering his, and then she dropped them in shame.

An unknown power had conquered her. Abercrombie could not resist taking her hand —only for a moment—but the moment lengthened, and neither of them spoke. At length, tears swam in Mercy's eyes; she drew her hand hastily away, and, before he could realize her intention, had fled from the room.

After that she avoided him. He had never a chance for one word with her ; but he had seen enough of Mercy to know that her heart must have been stirred to the very bottom ere her tears would have witnessed against her.

When she had left him, he stood irresolute ; then he covered his face with his hands like a man who prays, and wrung them together, struggling with his passion, walking to and fro in the room.

He felt that the ground whereon he stood was holy ground, and that the woman was sacred to him.

He knew he was a nobler man since the light of her life, with its purity and singleness of purpose, had shone upon his ; and the question pressed him sorely, would he not be happier and better if he were to put aside the conventional obstacles which stood in his way, abandon the commonplace life of a man-about-town with an enemy in the social position which he could not afford to sustain, and marry Mercy, if she would be his wife ?

Algernon fought a great battle. His foes were Pride and Prejudice ; and he believed himself a conquering hero, when at best he was but a vaunting coward, in deciding at last to go away in silence.

But he was a hero who felt like a thief. When remorse was added to his grief, he cajoled his kinder nature into calling his selfishness prudence.

It was the first time in his life that he had ever attempted to practice that questionable virtue. He was alarmed at his own earnestness, and, as time went by, he found himself almost mad with desire to possess the girl.

The morning he left the old house, he endeavored to speak with her alone ; but she, imagining that he had detected her feelings and pitied them, and ashamed of the grief which she could not hide, avoided him, so that he was obliged to say good-bye before the assembled family, where all—even the green parrot—joined in a noisy farewell.

He looked back as he was driven from the door, beseeching one loving glance, but she quickly turned away—a dreadful misery in her heart which she dared not utter to herself.

The old house was like a *morgue*. The very fish-nets were full of associations. The sunshine streamed into the room. She took Algie's palette upon her thumb, and, putting her arms around the easel, leaned upon it. She was so intense in all her feelings, that to be deprived of any one of the few things she loved deadened her with wretchedness, and it became labor to lift a hand or make a step. What did such suffering mean? She felt that she could not endure it for long. The pain in her heart came back, and the muscles of her throat choked her. She pressed her hands upon her side. She was feeling now for herself, the pain she had so often before suffered for others—only more—far more of it. It seemed as if it could only stop when the heart should stand still.

She threw herself on the lounge and pressed the pillow under her side, but the anguish continued.

Abercrombie, judging her by the reserve of her farewell, could not have believed that she could suffer so for him. How could he—how could any man—understand the distrust a woman feels of her ability to withstand temptation which makes her, in her effort to protect herself, do the very opposite of the thing she desires to do?

The woman in whom this instinct is lacking is incapable of virtue.

Abercrombie understood women as well as did most men of his age and experience, but it is impossible that any man should know women thoroughly, since in the two opposing natures the superlative virtues are courage to attack and integrity to defend.

The Captain, blissfully ignorant of Mercy's heartache at home, which he would have given all he owned in the world to heal, was excessively talkative and facetious as they jogged along to the station, Algie morosely silent and ill at ease. If their thoughts could have been known, a very ill-assorted pair they would have seemed.

The Captain was bubbling over with satisfaction, and, as soon as they reached Richmond, dragged Algie off to a framer's to choose a frame.

Algie wished it to be subservient to the picture ; but the Captain greeted his choice with a derisive jeer. "I ain't got but one child, and I choose fur her to have everything o' the *best !* " he said.

The shopkeeper agreed with the customer, and when the picture reached Blessington House, it shone like the dome of the Kremlin.

At the foot of Abercrombie's stairs they parted. The Captain held the young man's hand for a long time in his large, cordial grasp, urging him again and again to come back to Cassandra to see them all, adding that he knew Mercy would be "*more'n glad* to see him." And then he took out his red-silk handkerchief and blew his nose and went away, leaving Algie standing in the doorway, watching him till he was lost in the crowd.

Algie dreaded to think that that might be the last of Cassandra.

He thoughtfully ascended the stairs, expecting to be able to take up his old life again just where he had left it. But things did not seem the same to him. He missed the warmth of heart which had pervaded Blessington House. His rooms looked lonely and cold after the fluffy comfort of that humbler home.

It was a mild evening in May, but he felt chilly and ordered a fire.

His servant handed him a bundle of letters. Most of them were bills, some of them duns, so he put them away. His mind was too bruised from the recent conflict to confront a new perplexity.

He hurried the man about his work, and when he had finally dismissed him, though early in the evening, he locked the door, and sat down to rest his brain and assure himself that he had acted for the best. But the more he thought over his position, the less tenable it seemed. He longed to go back to Mercy, as to a tribunal of that grace whose name she bore, to tell her of his perplexities. He glanced at the unopened bills. Would she frown upon him and rebuke the enormity of his persistent carelessness ? Not that he was more criminal than most young men of fashion whose incomes are out of proportion to their position ; but most women, even the wives of such men, would think such neglect of effort to adjust expenditure to income, criminal.

He was honest enough not to commit the fallacy of cursing his luck ; he knew there was no luck about it. Stretched out in his chair and staring blindly at the clock, he felt like Prometheus bound, and longed to break away from the debts which threatened to devour his substance, and be free of the trammels of family pride and society, and live to suit himself.

Himself, as he looked that personage over, was a weak slave to the admiration of other men—a one-sided creature, leaning continually upon others. If he must lean upon another, why might not that other be Mercy, who was so strong to support those who needed moral co-operation ?

He wondered at his own infatuation for the girl. Her impalpable image seemed almost to touch his soul, and he dreaded to meet his own mother, for fear that her pleasantry might touch upon his love.

He took the little picture out of his portmanteau, and stood it up before the clock on the mantelpiece, and kissed it with an excess of tenderness, murmuring over it. Abercrombie was a particularly gentle man, and all these little acts were gently done, as if he were touching Mercy herself.

His reverie was full of poignant contrition. The intensest longing to implore her love and forgiveness rent his breast. The memory of the tears he had seen her shed scalded his heart as if they had been hot blood dropping upon it.

Algie was not vicious. Doubtless he was nobler than he knew,—liberal certainly, and extravagant to folly; but his extravagance consisted mainly in giving beyond what he could afford of his bread and meat, or rather of his champagne and terrapin.

He was tired of spending his money on those who cared nothing for him. He had come to an age when a man wants to be master of his own house, with his wife by his side and his child at her breast. He had done spending his energies and affections upon heartless idlers; he wanted to concentrate his devotion upon some one who loved him as well. Who was capable of loving him with such self-abnegation as Mercy? He would be a god to her if she loved him. He knew it. But—did she love him?

If she truly loved him, why was she so ashamed to let him look into her heart and see all? Her heart was so chaste, she need not have been ashamed of it.

Poor Mercy! Alas, wandering about the familiar marshes, her lagging steps led her nowhere; and so surely does any powerful emotion make us react upon our accustomed selves that she, whose self-abnegation had been almost ideal, felt as if doing good was a dead-and-gone possibility. She even talked to herself—laughing—practising little devices to amuse her father on his return, that he might not discover her secret.

All this time the Captain was at a second-rate hotel down near the docks, with his hat cocked on the back of his head, his spectacles shoved up against the rim, his big, smooth red face wreathed in smiles, bragging about the new brig ; while a crowd of familiar acquaintances, to whom he was standing treat, sat round a table with glasses of hot grog perpetually refilled.

Jack was there too, echoing the praises of the ship, until the old skipper slapped him on the back and swore that he was the happiest boy in Richmond town.

The next morning Abercrombie passed for the pink of prosperity as he walked about the streets and was congratulated upon his return to the city. When he reached his mother's door he let himself in and sought her unannounced. Some hours afterwards he came out again, but there was something different in his mien and the decision with which he stepped upon the pavement.

He had endeavored to make a confidante of his mother, and, although his confessions had been received with good nature, the half-bantering ridicule with which she had spoken of Mercy, of the old Captain, who, she had heard, "swallowed knives like an ostrich," and of the *preposterousness* of the whole idea, forced Algie to take his ground precipitately, perhaps, but resolutely, and for life. There had been no hard words on either side, but his mother realized with dismay that he really loved the girl, and that he meant to merit Mercy's confidence.

16

HE premature summer put new life into all nature at Cassandra. Floods of sunshine poured upon the sea until it glowed like one of Turner's pictures, but the broad stripes of ruby and sapphire did not rouse Mercy from the lethargy into which she had fallen. Even as a child she had been absent, as if self-mesmerized, with her eyes fixed vacantly and her mind far away; but now her brain was focussed upon one thought, and that thought was Abercrombie. He was lonely amid the distractions of a city; how much more lonely was she, bound by the monotony of her life to the perpetual repetition of trivial acts, each one of which was inseparable from her recollections of him.

That memory was more persistent than her own shadow: waking, she thought of him, sleeping, she dreamed of him. The pain in her side was incessant, and food became abhorrent to her.

Aunt Polly, preoccupied with her religion, did not observe that Mercy's color was fading and her cheeks sinking. Antonio watched his young mistress in silence, and his heart ached for her.

The fishermen shook their heads with mis-giving. "Somethin's a-ailin' our Mercy," they would say to one another, as they saw her follow her rounds languidly. They felt that the light upon their paths was dim. No one dared speak of it to the Captain. "She's a-follerin' her mother," some said, pointing to the graveyard and sighing.

But the Captain, blind in his fullness of generosity, rejoiced with the joy of a bene-factor. He was abounding in satisfaction at the pleasure he was giving Mercy through Jack, and had no eyes for the blue veins in her temples nor the thinness of her lower eye-lids ; neither did he observe how often she pressed her hand upon her heart.

Antonio saw it and was as silent as the grave. To none other than Mercy would he speak. *Should* he speak to her ? What could he do to help her if he did speak ? But at night, when Splugen and Bill Junk were sleeping their profound and healthy sleep, the little wizened old man would steal from his bed and get down on his knees in the corner, dimly lighted by the floating taper which burned of late before the image of " Our Lady," and pray to God and invoke the Saints and bribe the Blessed Virgin with the promise of innumerable worldly goods. These he offered to Her honor for the consolation of the distressed and the glory of Her dear Son,

if in the pity of Her heart she would intercede
for him that his prayers might be answered
—that Mercy, the joy of the house and the
angel of the poor, might be made happy
again, as she used to be. Then he would
cover the battered crucifix with kisses, his
withered lips trembling the while ; and again,
when despair seized him and earthly comfort
seemed of no avail, he would cry out : " O my
Jesu ! give her Thy heart as a pledge of Thy
love, as a place of refuge, wherein she may
find a secure repose during life, and a sweet
comfort in the hour of death ! Amen." The
despair of this thought would overpower him,
and he would weep in anguish, bowing himself upon the board floor. Then he would
creep noiselessly back to his bed, hoping for
the best.

One day Splugen brought a little flat package from the express-office. Antonio fetched
it to Mercy. She recognized Algie's hand-
writing, and trembled with such strange excitement that Antonio took it from her and
cut the cord. It contained a parcel of his
sketches, a water-color box, and some direc-
tions for sketching simple objects. It filled
her with a delight of which Algie could not
have dreamed. There was neither message
nor address. She could not thank him, but it
seemed to comfort her to know that he had
thought of her. When he had arranged the
package he had pictured her wandering about
the marshes, trying with characteristic per-

severance to lay in bits of sky and water.
She seized upon the suggestion. Abandoning
her books as companions on the sands, she
wandered no more like a young philosopher,
with an essay closed over her fingers, and her
mind full of the thoughts it had suggested.
Hope awoke in her breast, and she exerted
herself once more to be absorbingly interested
in the most trivial incidents about her. She
went more frequently to see Granny Gooch,
and forced herself to listen to her whinings.
Even such maunderings were better than the
gloom of her own thoughts. When the May
calms came she read every afternoon to the
children, and, the wind being lulled and the
sea still, only the lapping of the ground-swell
accompanied her voice. But even the children
felt that there was a meekness about her
which was different from the independence of
her old manner.

Granny Gooch became ashamed of complaining when Mercy made no reply.

Things went their way till, one bright day
in June, Jack came home. The brig was
ready. He had brought her down the river
on a trial trip, and all were to go and inspect
her as she lay in a little bay not far from Cassandra.

They arose early to avoid the heat. The
old gray horse was hitched to a small wagon,
end the Captain spread himself upon the front
seat, while Aunt Polly and Mercy occupied
the second. Mother Margery had been in-

vited, but at the last moment declined going, for she shrank painfully from Jack's farther seafaring. She constantly looked to the tree-tops, far inland, and sighed to abandon her cabin and the wreck-strewn shore.

Antonio kept the house. Bill Junk and Splugen followed the wagon on foot, while Jack walked beside it, with his hand on the rail, and his eyes from time to time wandering to Mercy's face. There was a strange look there which puzzled him, and he wondered more and more what it meant.

The girl, nevertheless, was making merry about the new ship, and talking to him as if life were a fairy-tale. But she was much too merry for Jack. He knew it was all a pretence: he had been merry lately himself. The Mercy of old would have been quiet under the importance of the event, and have dreaded his going to sea again. That morning, on the contrary, she was bantering and facetious, and it annoyed him—he could scarcely tell why. He wished she were silent and thoughtful, for he did not feel merry; and her gaiety had something pathetic about it. When Mercy laughed, involuntarily he felt like weeping. He had learned that it was a serious thing to go to sea and be responsible for the lives and sufferings of other men.

"So you reconciled yourself to the name I chose, after all, did you, Jack?" said she, smiling at him: he had been looking so solemnly at her.

" Yes," said Jack.

" Why didn't you like it at first ? The ' Pansy ' sounds quite original," said she.

" I fear it savors a little of the Johnny Jump-up ! "

Mercy looked astonished at hearing Jack make a pun. " I had thought of it rather as a heart's-ease to you, Jack," she said, with such a tender inflection in her voice that he started.

There was a helpless look of appeal in Mercy's eyes when they met his. It reminded him of the pink curlew which had fallen at his feet, and he felt an unintelligible but gloomy presentiment arise in his mind. What was hurting her ? Surely there was a wound somewhere which he could not see. Why should she be so anxious to give him the ship ?—for he knew very well that she had per-suaded her father to do it—and why had she so insisted upon naming it for the flower with this complexity of names ? A " Pansy " that should be a " Heart's-ease " to him, and " Johnny Jump-up " to signalize his promotion. It was at once pathetic and comical.

Did she think she was going to die of that pain in her heart ? Jack shuddered at the thought. Then it occurred to him that she wished his ambition to supplant his love.

He continued to walk in silence, with his eyes fixed upon the ground. What was the meaning of that tone of tenderness which could only have been generated by suffering ?

Was she pitying him ? Alas ! it seemed the sympathy of one in despair.

Was Mercy's heart yearning as sadly for another as his yearned for her ? Who was that other ? He could think of none but Abercrombie, and the more he thought of it the more natural it seemed to him that Mercy should love so accomplished and attractive a man. Thinking of Algie, Jack despised himself. He felt as if he were the great rough-hewn block of a statue, and Algie was the finished work. Thus thinking, he looked again at Mercy.

She had forgotten him, forgotten Aunt Polly, grim and severe beside her ; forgotten her father, big and prosperous and imposing before her ; forgotten the fair blue sky above, and the white sands beneath her feet ; forgotten the Carolina turtle-doves cooing in the bushes, and the masts of the brig in the distance ; forgotten the whole world, and allowed the pain to creep out and paint itself in gray lines upon her face ; and Jack, who loved her so, who might have been so happy that day if he had not loved her, was compelled to keep silence, trying to think out, with so few premises, what it could all be about. Because he was so certain, by the intuition of a fellow-feeling, that Algie loved her, it did not seem possible it could have come from a want of that love.

She suddenly remembered herself, looked at Jack uneasily, and met his eyes (those big brown eyes with a hot fire glowing in them), and spiritually crouched before him like a guilty thing. \

She struggled to seem indifferent, but the struggle was too visible. She had made the effort valiantly, and the pathetic failure was more pitiful to Jack than any amount of weeping or complaining.

He saw it was a sorrow he could never hope to heal by himself, but he might find a means to do so through the instrumentality of another. Could he devise a means to reach that other ?

He recalled the morning, two months ago, when he had told Mercy the story of the wreck ; how he had said to her that he believed he could die for her, or die even to save the life of a man she loved, if he thought it would be the means of making her happy. Could he not now throw himself into the breach and mend the rent between them ?

Could she be happy if he, Jack, were dead or gone ? That possibility was more bitter than the thought of death, for Jack stood in no great fear of death.

He looked at her again ; and again she had forgotten him ; forgotten him this day, the last for many weeks which they should spend together. The longing from which she could not escape possessed her, and Jack realized that he was outside of her life, of that secret inner life which is as lonely as the soul at death.

They were entering the long town skirting
the water. A confusion of masts and tangled
cordage edged the shore, and hundreds of
little boats were gently rocking in the hollows
of the waves. The waters of the bay were
like a sheet of pale green glass, transparently
beautiful. A rosy mist hung over the sea.
But neither Jack nor Mercy seemed to be
alive to the beauty of the day. Jack had hoped
to be glad, and, instead, his heart was heavier
than before ; Mercy's heart ached because she
hoped for nothing at all. It did not seem
possible to her that Algie could care for her,
when he must be constantly meeting dozens
of women much more finished and charming.
Could he possibly cherish one thought of her
among her rough people ? They seemed
rough to her now. She missed him and felt
the contrast.

The Captain was in a gale of high spirits,
and had a joke for every old tar on the wharf.

Mercy and Jack exerted themselves to make
the day go off merrily.

The " Pansy's " boat came off with feather-
ing oars and took them all out to the brig.
Splugen crowded in the full hampers for the
day's repast, and when the boat touched, the
Captain climbed the rope-ladder over the
brig's sides. Aunt Polly followed, assisted by
Splugen. Jack and Mercy went after them.

The shadow of the flag fell upon the deck.
" Long may she wave ! " said Jack.

The " Pansy " was not less beautiful than her

name. The sun gleamed on her yellow decks, and glinted amid the shadows of the shrouds on her masts, and flashed as if meteors were imprisoned in the galley rails, and the brass knobs of the companion-way ; the compass-box defied the sun itself for splendor, and radiant in blueness, like a hollow sapphire, glowed the sky, and dazzling as an emerald was the sea.

Jack and Mercy, leaning over the bulwarks, watched the sailors haul up the boat and swing it over the revolving davits.

Mercy became so enlivened with the bustle that she forgot her wretchedness, and after a while, sitting down upon a coil of rope, watched the bowsprit rock this way and that, amid the entanglement of spars and cordage, until she became dizzy herself.

The scene and the thought of Jack's prosperity had undoubtedly wrought a temporary change in her feelings, and Jack himself, who reflected Mercy's moods, felt the contrast. A delirious wish formed in his mind. What a glad life it would be to have Mercy at his side, and roam with her the far and lonely seas, in delicious isolation ; her true heart forever near his breast, that thus, all and all to each other, they might live and die.

Alas, he was mad with a folly all his own ! But he was happy for one day with his desire fulfilled ; and Mercy looked at him with pleasure in her eyes, satisfied to think that he was pleased with the ship.

The day was all too short. Jack would have riveted the sun in the top of the sky if he could, that it might never go down; but slowly it sank lower and lower. A breeze had sprung up; there could be no excuse to keep them over night on board; and the time came for the Captain to gather up his people and depart, after wishing Jack "God-speed."

Aunt Polly and Splugen were already climbing over the bulwarks, with a mixture of grotesque gallantry and antique feminine coquettishness. One must admit it takes very pretty feet, to say the least of it, to climb a rope-ladder down the side of a ship, and drop off into a boat on the swell of the sea.

The Captain was already in the boat, having set himself for ballast, but Jack and Mercy were still below in the cabin of the brig. Perhaps Jack had timed it so.

Mercy was taking her last look around. The narrow doors to the bunks on either side were closed. The ugly little black stove crouched in the corner beamed with leaden lustre, the table at one side was covered with a red cloth, the pale green walls ornamented with a golden rod, the hanging-lamp ready to be lighted, and the book-case, in another corner, filled with books. Ah! Mercy would never forget that scene, nor Jack standing before her,—his face glowing with color, his profusion of chestnut hair, his gently arched black eyebrows, his eloquent eyes timid with

an unuttered wish, all were impressed upon
her memory forever.

"Mercy, I hate so for you to leave me,"
said he, taking her hand with the familiarity
which had existed between them since their
childhood. "Won't you tell me what troubles
you before you go?—before I go? Surely
there is something hurting you deeply, and
you are keeping it back from me. It is because you can't understand me, Mercy. You
don't know how utterly I love you—how all
that the world holds of joy or happiness or
life are locked up in you. Sometimes I wish
I had never come back, I should have been
spared so much. I should have lost this
happy day, but also this unutterable pain of
separation, for it is like tearing my soul out
of my body; and the hardest part of all is to
leave you suffering. To feel that a sorrow
which is your own has come between us. If
it were joy it would not be so hard. Tell me,
Oh, tell me, my darling, what it is?"

But Mercy listened without moving or
speaking. Jack still held her hand. It was
pulseless and cold. He waited in pleading
silence, but her lips were rigid. She looked
at him. There was infinite trust in her eyes,
but it was impossible for her to speak.

"You will not tell me; you used to tell me
everything," he said, regretfully.

"Oh, Jack, I cannot tell. I do not know."

He paused a moment hesitating. At last he
said, "But I know, Mercy, and I am certain

that he loves you ; and I swear to you it shall
all come right. You know my superstition
that I was saved from the wreck to save you
from something ; God only knows what, but
if you will trust me, I will do it ; and I will
find a way to make you happy. I hear them
calling ; let me kiss you good-bye as I always
have done, once more, only once more, dear
Mercy. I promise you I will make you happy
at any cost, if I must die to do it."

Without waiting her denial, he put his loving arm around her and kissed her tenderly,
as if she had been a sacred thing, and then
sprang through the companion-way, and was
gone.

But her heart stood still, and her cheeks
burned red because he kissed her. Never
till that moment had she realized her self-
consecration to another, and she trembled
with such agitation that she clung to the rail
to support herself.

Jack returned to the skylight and called
her, but she shrank from his gaze when they
met. He was holding her hand to steady her
over the bulwark : " Dear Mercy, forgive me,
I love you so," he whispered ; and as she
looked at him she saw the same look in his
eyes that had been in Algie's own, that last
day in May when she had fled from him.
Jack's words had told the meaning of it. " *I
love you so*," he said.

At the wharf Jack left them, after a lingering " Good-bye," and many times repeated

"God bless you," and "Luck to ye," was shouted after him across the water.

They watched the sailors hoist the boat, and swing it up, and lash it over the poop, heard the grating of the chains as they weighed anchor, heard Jack's voice in command, and Mercy forgot, for the moment, the tones of the lover, as she heard him ordering his men to and fro. They saw the mainsail unfurled and the gaff hoisted high, and the white canvas spread on the breeze. There was a light wind, and all the square sails and jibs too were put out.

The "Pansy" toyed with the water, rocking to and fro, as if coquetting with her image in a glass, and then she moved just a little, very slowly, her sails rounding more and more, until they shifted the tack, and she glided suddenly away like a beautiful, home-loving bird, with her white wings spread. The crowd on the shore cheered and waved. All the villagers were there, and they waved and cheered, and waved again! The Captain pulled out his great red handkerchief and flung it at arm's length. Jack, although so brave, dropped his arm in terror. Who knows what he thought, but it was a blood-red flag over Mercy's head. He had all a sailor's superstitions. He knew no fear of realities which he could fight, but of the unseen, unknown, unconquerable, he had a nameless dread.

The Captain saw the sudden dropping of

Jack's arm, and after a moment he wiped his brow in perplexity and shook his head gravely, saying : " Well, I'll be damned ! "

I fear the recording angel, who wept over Uncle Toby's oath, would make a blistered page of the Captain's long account. I can but think that the milk of human kindness, which came ever welling from his good old heart, must have washed out all the venom ere the many bad words he uttered escaped his unguarded lips.

" He's afeard o' your red handkercher ! " said an old tar, touching the Captain's arm.

"Good Lord, man," cried the Captain, amazed, " what's there to be afeard o' in that ! "

But Splugen supplied him with a tablecloth, and they all joined hands on it, and waved and shouted till the vessel was too far away to answer their signals, and they were forced to desist.

A little later they were plodding along over the sands by the way they had come. Jack was gone. The new brig was no fiction ; the day was done ; and Mercy went home, more silent than before.

CHAPTER XIX.

HEN Algie returned to his studio, after the interview with his mother, the gentleman of fashion and elegant leisure was left outside, and only the natural man entered, prepared to grapple with his difficulties and vanquish them.

His mind, habituated to commenting coldly upon his emotions, wondered at the power which had arisen in his breast, and demanded co-operation from itself.

Was Algie a hero after all ? Did he truly wish to put aside the temptations of the world, its adulation, which more than all things he had loved, its luxury and thoughtless ease ?

To what purpose ?

He sat thinking for a few moments ; then he opened his bills, looked over the items, added them up, separately and *in toto ;* and finally revolved in his mind the various possible means of paying them.

" I shall go into exile," said he with a sigh, which seemed rather of relief, as of a resolute man who has his enemy at last, and considers how to dispose of him.

17

The sum of money was large relatively. He could not go to his mother for help. She would have the right to laugh at him—though she had often before paid dearly for that privilege.

He took out his pocket-book containing the check which the Captain had given him. There was something in the big, ignorant signature which smote his heart. How could he use it as a thing of trade, or take pay in any form, for the dear pleasure of painting Mercy's portrait ! It seemed like money obtained upon a false pretext. He looked at the bills again.

They had not shrunk.

"Five bouquets at five dollars each ! " he ejaculated. " Dance with a girl that you care nothing about, pay five dollars for her flowers, and feel all the time that she is measuring you by their merits, and not for your own." Had he really ever loved any woman before to the intrinsic value of a dozen cut roses or one orchid ?

He had never offered Mercy a flower ; but he loved her ; he felt certain of it. He measured his love, not by etiquette, but by the sacrifices he was willing to make for it.

" One dozen China silk handkerchiefs, name embroidered in white," he continued. " Of course they might have been marked in ink, but that is so vulgar and conspicuous."

" Three baskets of champagne—one hundred and five dollars. To be sure ! " That

was for his New-Year supper. They had had a
gorgeous time unquestionably, and one fellow,
happier than the rest, had stood on his head
upon the table ; and all had finished by holding each other's coat-tails, and singing glorious
songs, marching around the festive board.
He had had enough of that sort of thing.

There had been no bills since he went to
Cassandra. It was the 31st of March, he
remembered. On that day the tide of his life
had turned. By a singular coincidence, Jack's
life had been in deadly peril upon the same
day.

Algie got up and walked the floor.

A great desire seized him to go to the old
Captain, and fling himself into his bountiful
heart, as if it had been a gulf, full, like the sea,
of goodness and generosity, and say to the
listening compassion which should encompass
him : "Forgive me. I love your child, your
darling. Consider my past delinquencies, but
also my temptations. Help me, care for me,
even feed me, until I can pay my debts out of
my income, and I will do all I can for you in
return ! "

Alas ! He stood on his pride and rejected
the thought.

If he had done so, the Captain would have
taken down his spectacles and looked at him,
have grumbled a little, which was his only
privilege, and then he would have flourished
the red handkerchief and considered ; and,
finally, would have taken Algie into the

securest nook of the great heart, and have anchored him there alongside of Mercy. And then he would have treated him like a superior being, and have bragged about him, as he did about everything he loved and doted on. And Mercy, save for her sympathy in Jack's disappointment, would have been happy.

But Algie was too much of a man to do any such childish thing ; so, full of his conceit, he got a large atlas and looked at a little dot marked " Cassandra Bay."

He meant to lock up these unhome-like rooms, and go somewhere to sketch and economize. He would buckle himself down to hard work ; and, by the compensation of labor, lose his natural desire for amusement. He would begin afar off—but Blessington House should be the ultimate goal of his pilgrimage.

He concluded to borrow money upon collateral to pay his debts, and then go and grind for weeks and months, if need be, until the amount should be refunded. He would not attempt to possess himself of the luxury of a wife until his debts were paid.

He ignored the fact that the luxury he was denying himself was a human being, capable of intensest suffering and disappointment, and also of paying the debts.

The day before he left to enter into his penitential exile, he had sent Mercy the package of sketches and notes, but not a word of explanation or kindness. He had, it is true, written a few words to Aunt Polly, as the mistress of Blessington House, thanking her for her kindness during his stay there, but to Mercy he had not sent a line.

As the days followed one another, Algie, full of the sincerity of his intentions, became happier, and his health was improved by his life in the open air.

All day long he dreamed of the home he meant to make, with Mercy for his bride.

" Surely she loves me," he said to himself, remembering the quiver of her lip and the tears in her eyes ; and moreover had she not told him that she was "one of those dreadful people who never forget." She must love him still, for he had done nought to wound her. He would not wound a hair of her head. Was there nothing to hurt her in the silence which he would not vouchsafe to explain ?

*   *   *   *   *

A good many months had passed in this fashion, and October frost had nipped the grass, browned the leaves of the scrub oaks, and blackened the cedars, ere Algie reached a little village not far from Cassandra Bay.

He walked with the jaunty air and buoyant step of a free man, as he followed the path which meandered through the rushes, among which the tide ponds gleamed.

He could hear the distant boom of the ocean, and that, as well as the smell of the marsh, brought back to him the sunny April days.

His heart beat with passionate expectation, and tears almost of rapture moistened his eyes as the old red walls of Blessington House came in view. Never had he been so glad to get anywhere, or see anything, as he felt at sight of the grim pile which stood out against the sky like a coastguard station.

His heart beat with a moment's uncertainty as he put up his hand to open the gate. He found the three sailors asleep in the garden, with their chairs tilted against the wall of the house.

Sailor growled, but, upon recognizing him, wagged his tail and whined with satisfaction.

The parrot screamed until she wakened Antonio.

"At last," said the old man, upon perceiving Algie, " Our Lady has answered me ! "

Algie shook hands with the men all around. They told him that he looked " oncommon well." Any picturesque dress was becoming to him ; and the blue-flannel shirt, and velveteen breeches belted with a fair leather strap, showed his well-made figure to advantage. His coat was hanging over his arm.

" Are the family upstairs ? " asked Algie.

" No, sir, nobody but Miss Polly," answered Bill Junk, who was always the loquacious one of the three. " Miss Mercy ain't bin peert fur a good while, and she an' the skipper is gone out a-walkin' down to Jack's. Ef ye'll

jest step up an' set a while, one o' us'll go
fetch 'em," indicating Splugen, who did the
errands for the house.

"Oh, no, thank you ! Not by any means,"
cried Algie, and fearing he had been overheard, he hurried out of the gate, closing it
firmly behind him.

CHAPTER XX

LGIE enjoyed the stiff breeze, and found it bracing and pleasant after his walk.

"Miss Mercy ain't been peert lately," he repeated to himself, "but, she's off at Jack's! Just what I might have expected! Curse the luck of it! I wish I had come back before."

He pulled his moustache as he sauntered along, scanning the distance, and listening for voices. "It's chilly for her to be out if she's ill. I wonder the old man takes so little care of her," he mused.

When he arrived at the divergent path which led to Mother Margery's cabin, he hesitated. Anxious as he was to see Mercy, he had some compunction about seeking her under Jack's very roof.

He stood vacillating, kicking the sand, uncertain whether to follow that path or another which led off to the north. The latter was obscure and unpromising; but, being unwilling that Jack should witness his meeting with Mercy, he took it.

As he walked along, idly looking about him,

he was enraptured with the beauty of the marshes, glowing in the sunset with many luminous shades of green, while the water amid the grasses gleamed with red and purple, reflected from the sky.

When he finally came out upon the bluff overlooking the beach, he wondered that Mercy had never brought him there, for it was much the most beautiful spot along the coast. The sands were spaciously wide and flat, and the bluff unusually high.

The tide was coming in so fast, it would not be long ere the water would cover the broad stretch to the foot of the cliff.

There was one place in the sands which seemed different from all the rest, gleaming with silvery lustre, while the other sands were rosy, or yellow and white, and winding out from the cliff like a sullen serpent creeping to the sea.

This so excited Algie's curiosity that he followed the bluff until he reached a place shelving enough to admit of his climbing down.

Having done so, he walked along the beach, crunching the shells under his feet. The sea-gulls were flying low, screaming their shrill good-nights. As he wandered on, picking up small objects of interest here and there, he forgot the singular sand which he had come to examine, and advanced to meet the surf, throwing sticks into the sea and watching them sweeping in again amidst the foam on the wave's edge, which spread sideways like the feathers on a lady's opening fan. Pausing, he watched the foam turn red as it churned up the powdered shells ; until, attempting to move forward, he was surprised to find that his feet were so heavy that it was almost impossible to lift them.

He bent all his strength to lift his right foot ; but, although he succeeded, his dismay was unutterable to find that his other foot had sunk much deeper, and that the sand was oozing in at his shoetops.

"What can be the matter?" thought Algie, feeling rather amused than alarmed, but nevertheless stretching his loose foot as far back as possible from the foam of the advancing wave. But all of a sudden there came to him the memory of a chance allusion to the quicksand on the North Beach.

An indescribable horror blanched his face, and made him throw up his hands with a gesture of despair.

Had he been less panic-stricken, and remembered the silvery stream of talc-like lustre which he had come down from the cliff to investigate, he would have recollected how narrow it was, as it crawled out from the cliff ; but his presence of mind forsook him, and he guided his struggling steps backward, instead of sideways, bewildered by the terror he felt of the rapidly incoming tide, which was upon him.

Each struggling step backward took him

deeper into the sands, for they were becoming slimier with the access of the sea.

Physically, Algie was not strong at best, and his entire body, already wet with perspiration from the effort he was making, now began to relax, and spasmodically the muscles refused to move. He had a courageous heart, and, having realized his extremity, endeavored to meet it as nobly as he could. His mind was alert, but it became moment by moment more difficult to sustain the physical effort which he was obliged to make. He dared not pause, even an instant, to look around, for each time that he succeeded in releasing one foot, the other sank deeper, and it was more difficult to withdraw it. Moreover, he began to realize that an appalling paralysis was overpowering him.

At last his strength was entirely gone. The tide was rolling in, and the spray made him shiver. He had sunk to his knees.

In the agony of despair he abandoned his efforts and looked about him. Not a creature was in sight. He felt that he was being sucked in slowly, and the tide was rising inevitably ; but his mind was more heroic than he had believed of himself. He would fight for life, if only enough of life to fulfil what he had left undone ; he would tell Mercy that he had not meant to neglect her nor wished to forget her. Then his conscience would be at rest.

In this last agony there seemed no hope for

himself. He yelled for help, but the wind was blowing so hard it drowned his cries. He struggled again and dragged his legs some way along, for the sand was a little looser than at first. Then he felt himself going down, down, suddenly faster. Everything was giving way under his feet.

*   *   *   *   *

Not long after Algie's departure from Blessington House, Mercy returned, accompanied by her father and Jack. Antonio, eager to make her happy, was ready at the gate with the news; and Jack, looking into Mercy's face, saw it overspread with a glow of ineffable joy. It was a death-blow to Jack's own hopes, but the sorrow was without reproach in the kind look of his eyes, as they searched with inquiry into Mercy's own.

"I will go and fetch him," said he, anxious to make her happy, even at such cost to himself.

Had Algie been as single-hearted as poor Jack, he would not now be struggling in the slough of such despair.

Mercy blushed painfully at finding her heart thus open to Jack's inquiry, and turned away abashed, unable to answer him. He was about to go, when he suddenly placed himself before her, and with a loving look, which she never afterwards forgot, took her hand in his and said in a whisper: "Can't you believe, dear Mercy, that I love you more than I love myself?"

Then he hurried out of the gate and across the marshes to a spot where three paths met. When he scrutinized the freshly-trodden footprints, there was a place where some one had halted, kicking the sands carelessly, and finally seemed to have turned to the northward by the dangerous way which skirted the bluff and edged the quicksand.

Anxiety made Jack hasten, but when he reached the bluff and looked around, at first he saw nothing amiss. The sun had set, but it was brightly light, for the full moon, new-risen in the east, flooded the beach with effulgent splendor.

He was looking admiringly up and down, his gaze lingering upon the sweeps of sand which glowed under the combined lights of sunset and moonrise, when something attracted his attention moving in the edge of the foam.

At first he thought it was a great bird—a southern pelican flapping its wings against its sides. The quicksand, with its snake-like winding, gleamed behind it. He fixed his gaze, for the object was indistinct and his eyes were dazed with watching the moonrise. But all at once he understood.

It was the head and arms of a human being! The sands had swallowed his body and were still sucking in the little visible portion of the miserable creature. The tide, also, was closing upon him with deadly certainty.

"My God!" cried Jack, "the man must be the painter, who has gone to his death—and Mercy's heart will break!"

He sprang down the sand-bluff and ran across the beach.

Alas! what help was there? Not a beam, nor rope's end, nor splinter of the debris the waves were ever bringing.

"Try and keep moving," cried Jack, coming nearer to Algie, and searching madly for something wherewith to reach him.

Algie was almost blind from exhaustion. He had sunk so low that the sands were pressing upon his breast, crushing the breath out of him, and they were driven by each successive breaker with the force of a renewed shock. The muscles of his chest could no longer resist the compression. He was as one in a mould which was setting.

When Jack called to him, he had so nearly lost consciousness that his interest in life was gone along with it. Jack dared not leave him to seek for help. In ten minutes the tide would be over his head and all be ended forever.

Jack tore off his clothes and tied them together with a sailor's deftness, and flung the end of the line to Algie. But Algie could not reach it; he had no strength left to push forward, even with such powerful help so near at hand.

"Are you still sinking?" cried Jack to him.

" No, I think not," replied Algie with difficulty.

" Can't you move a little toward me ? Oh,
try ! In a moment you may be drowned, and
Mercy——" Alas ! poor Jack, he was fren-
zied with despair for her as well as compassion
for Algie. To see almost within grasp a
human life which in a moment might be
annihilated !—a life which, Jack declared to
himself, held all of Mercy's happiness. Despair crazed him or drove him to that madness of courage which puts a man outside of
every instinct of self-preservation.

Desperate for an expedient, he sought all
about for some *small* piece of wood even. At
last he found a peg, and, going as near to the
edge of the quicksand as would bear his
weight, he pressed it firmly into the ground
and tied the line of clothes to it.

Again he flung the end of the line to Algie,
but again it was not long enough. Jack stood
erect one moment to think.

Algie, revived by Jack's encouragement, or
with a ruling passion strong in death, looked
with admiring eyes upon Jack's body as he
stood in the light of the moon, distinct against
the evening sky. The figure of a god, it
seemed so perfect, his flesh luminous, and
his eyes glowing with the warmth of a devotion which Algie thought divine.

Jack paused for an instant and cried out to
Algie: "I trust your honor. There's a
chance of one life between us ; whichever

wins, his life belongs to Mercy. I divide with you that chance !"

Algie, revived at this possibility, saw Jack take the line in his hands, and, lying down, stretch his body stiff, and roll with difficulty across the quicksand toward himself. Jack strained to reach Algie, but though his hands touched him, he had not grasp enough to clutch him, without letting go the line.

"For God's sake, struggle towards me !" cried Jack. Algie did his uttermost, but was so tight in the sands that he could not move.

Jack shuddered with terror. What if they both should die thus !

He lifted his eyes for another look at the dear land he was exchanging for a loathsome grave ; and then, without hope for himself, but braving the frightful death, he let go his hold of the line, and kneeling upon the sand, into which he speedily sank, he thrust his powerful arms under Algie's shoulders, clasped them around him, and with the help of Algie's feeble efforts, lifted him bodily out of the sands, while he, poor Jack, sank down in his place.

"Lean on me ! Only lean on me," cried Jack, with heroic self-immolation, "and stretch yourself out as straight and stiff as you can. Surely God will let us live till the tide comes in ;" and he watched the foam gather round him, whilst he sank faster and faster under the burden of Algie, borne upon his shoulders.

"Fling yourself sideways on the breaker, and remember, it is for Mercy's sake that I give you my life."

Algie, confused by the tumult in his mind, and dazed by the terrors he had gone through, only vaguely understood, at the time, the words which Jack had uttered; although the instinct of self-preservation made him cling to Jack's shoulder.

God only knows what heroes feel when they die: there are so few! But they seem to cast aside the poverty of the flesh, as if it were verily but rags hiding the immortal spirit. Who wonders that the heathen adored and apotheosized them, feeling it impossible that such godliness should cease at death or fail of its glory.

At last a great breaker burst over them, and wrenching Algie from Jack's upholding arms, shoved him along the surface of the quicksand, and left him upon the skirt of the shelly beach.

Then Jack was free to fight for his life. He gasped for breath, for the water had been over him, and struggled to regain the line. He had touched it. In a moment more he could have grasped it firmly, but another great breaker came and swept it far beyond his reach.

Algie's arms were palsied. He could not lift the line, nor fling it to Jack, who was drowning, with the surf breaking over his head.

18

Again and again Algie tried, but he could not move. His body was rigid with cramps, and was only a prison to his agonized spirit.

Jack strangled. Algie could hear the gurgling as he listened with bated breath. In his despair at not being able to save him, Algie would have died with him, and endeavored to throw himself into the quicksand, but a breaker promptly rolled him back.

And so Jack died, fulfilling the prophecy of his superstition, and making good the assurance which, out of the generosity of his heart, he had given Mercy, that he loved her so well that he believed he could die to save the life of a man she loved.

*　　　*　　　*　　　*　　　*

And while this frightful tragedy was being enacted a child had been running toward Blessington House. Speechless from fright, gasping for breath, and with her little hand upon her heart, she rushed against the Captain—who was promenading the garden-walk, impatiently awaiting Algie—his thumbs thrust into the armholes of his waistcoat, and his hat on the back of his head.

It was the same child that Jack had carried in his arms and warned against the sands on the day of his father's funeral.

" The sands, the sands ! " gasped she.

" Good Lord," cried the Captain, " what sands do ye mean ? "

" A man's in the sands ! The quicksands," cried the child.

Mercy, listening at the open window, and with a beating heart expecting Algie, certain that Jack would bring him back, overheard the child.

She listened for a moment incredulous, and then with a wail of terror fled out of the house and past the Captain, still parleying with the little girl.

All the household, but half understanding why they went, pursued her along the path by which Jack had followed Algie, and came out upon the cliff where Algie and Jack successively had stood.

Something like a log lay in the foam which the breakers were shoving ashore. Mercy climbed down the cliff and ran toward it, discovering that it was the body of a man.

When she had turned the face to the moonlight she saw Algie, but could not tell if he breathed.

Tearing the shirt from his breast, she pressed her ear against his flesh. The heart was faintly beating. Overcome by her grief, she pressed him, wet and cold, in her arms.

The others, hurrying after, took him away from her, and removed him beyond the reach of the tide. Finding that he was alive, they scanned the beach for Jack.

" It's strange we don't see nothin' on him," some one said, whilst they were endeavoring to restore Algie.

One of the men presently espied a long

black line shoved about amid the foam, and examined it.

A sailor's clothes, knotted together, and tied to a peg on the edge of the quicksand. Where could the man be? Who was he? Could he have sunk in the sands? Surely not Jack, who knew their danger well.

But when Algie came to, the wretched truth was disclosed, and all standing there felt dumb under the dreadful blow. Without a word, they stood watching the flood tide spread a silvery sheet over where Jack lay.

" My God, man, you'll have to do a lot o' good in this here worl' to cost sich a price ! " cried the Captain, merciless in the bitterness of his grief.

Mercy pressed Algie closer, in the pity of her heart, but she knew that what her father had said was true.

The men stood staring at the sea, incredulous.

" It could not be ! " they thought. " Jack dead ! "

Jack, the pride of master and men ; a few minutes before erect in the splendor of manhood, now laid low, and put out of sight forever, by the combined infernal devilment of land and sea ! "

Mercy knew it was true. She alone knew that Jack had superstitiously looked forward to the necessity of dying for her. He had told her so again and again ; many memories swept through her brain with a great rush.

She recalled the argument with Algie about the immortality of Jack's courage ; and the bitter question came to her : " Has Algie one quality as noble as Jack's love for me, or his devotion to his fellow-men ? "

Her judgment answered " *No*," but because of something great and generous in herself, she pressed Algie more closely in her arms, feeling that she had strength to do for him all that Jack had done for her.

THE END.

JEROME K. JEROME'S BOOKS